Praise for the Captain

'Arturo Pérez-Reverte['s] Alatriste books have sold more than five million copies worldwide' *Sunday Telegraph*

'A thinking man's adventure novel, where sword fights and tales of derring-do are interwoven with wonderful passages of poetry and gems of historical and cultural information' *The Times*

'Pérez-Reverte is very good at evoking the atmosphere of a teeming, corrupt and jaded Madrid, unhappily enduring the reign of Philip the Fourth in the last decades of Spain's imperial glory. He is superb at the precisely choreographed sword fights' *Daily Telegraph*

'Equipped with a quick-witted, charismatic hero and much to provoke and goad him, Mr Pérez-Reverte has the makings of a flamboyantly entertaining series. *Captain Alatriste* ends with a wicked flourish, an evil laugh and a strong likelihood that the best is yet to come' *New York Times*

'From the 19th century on, readers searching for adventure have always loved tales of flashing steel, of duels to the death on moonlit parapets, of swash-bucklers with ironic smiles and perfect manners . . . Arturo Pérez-Reverte now adds Captain Alatriste'

Washington Post

'Splendidly paced and filled with a breathtaking but not overwhelming sense of the history and spirit of the age, this is popular entertainment at its best: the characters have weight and depth, the dialogue illuminates the action as it furthers the story and the film-worthy plot is believable throughout' *Publishers Weekly*

'Pérez-Reverte's moody, wounded semi-hero . . . is a whole-cloth invention out of 17th-century Madrid that has led to a 21st-century literary phenomenon . . . introduces a charismatic, complicated leading man . . . the clash and dash are thrilling; the swordplay is a bonus' *Entertainment Weekly*

'*Purity of Blood* is the latest in a line of utterly unputdownable novels by Arturo Pérez-Reverte in which he has finessed a storytelling tradition stretching back to his great literary predecessors . . . This latest book is brimming with all the panache of previous novels by the writer and with even more confidence . . . this is glorious stuff, the kind of book to remind us how exhilarating old-fashioned adventure writing can be'
Daily Express

'Captivating . . . This is fiction that can be enjoyed on several levels: as a poignant evocation of doomed imperial splendour; as a clever literary game in which historical and invented figures rub shoulders; as a parable about racism past and present; or as a simple tale of swashbuckling derring-do' *Sunday Times*

'Intelligent, exciting historical swashbucklers . . . With writing rich in the minutiae of 17th-century Madrid life and interspersed with poetry, the author is clearly having a ball and the reader can join with him'
Waterstone's Books Quarterly

'Rich in historical detail and sardonic observations'
Publishers Weekly

'The plot moves quickly . . . Pérez-Reverte is . . . engaged with the theme of religious fanaticism, providing vivid depictions of the Inquisition and its public theatre of auto-da-fe'
Times Literary Supplement

'The book is full of vivid scenes bringing to life 17th-century Spain' *Sunday Telegraph*

'A worthy successor to Zorro and Scaramouche . . . he is knowledgeable and convincing in his evocation of those earlier, darker times . . . His novels are fine examples of historical writing for a mass audience, and that is his most important achievement' *Herald*

Arturo Pérez-Reverte lives near Madrid. Originally a war correspondent, he now writes fiction full time. His novels have been translated into thirty-four languages and published in more than fifty countries. In 2003 he was elected to the Spanish Royal Academy. Visit his website at www.perez-reverte.com

By Arturo Pérez-Reverte

The Flanders Panel
The Dumas Club
The Seville Communion
The Fencing Master
The Nautical Chart
The Queen of the South
Captain Alatriste
Purity of Blood
The Sun Over Breda
The Painter of Battles
The King's Gold
The Man in the Yellow Doublet
Pirates of the Levant

THE SUN
OVER BREDA

ARTURO PÉREZ-REVERTE

PHOENIX

A PHOENIX PAPERBACK

First published in Great Britain in 2007
by Weidenfeld & Nicolson
This paperback edition published in 2008
by Phoenix,
an imprint of Orion Books Ltd,
Orion House, 5 Upper St Martin's Lane,
London WC2H 9EA

An Hachette UK company

3 5 7 9 10 8 6 4 2

A CIP catalogue record for this book
is available from the British Library.

ISBN 978-0-7538-2360-6

Printed and bound in Great Britain by
Clays Ltd, St Ives plc

The Orion Publishing Group's policy is to use papers
that are natural, renewable and recyclable products and
made from wood grown in sustainable forests. The logging
and manufacturing processes are expected to conform to
the environmental regulations of the country of origin.

www.orionbooks.co.uk

For Jean Schalekamp
damned heretic,
interpreter and friend

A troop of soldiers marches by:
strong, bearded, weapons shouldered,
following their captain's lead.

Spanish captain, who knew Flanders,
Mexico, Italy, and the Andes,
Of what exploits are left to dream?

C.S. del Río
La esfera

THE SUN OVER BREDA

1. SURPRISE ATTACK

Pon my oath, the canals of these Dutch are damp on autumn mornings. Somewhere above the curtain of fog that veiled the dike, a blurred sun shone palely on the silhouettes moving along the road in the direction of the city, now opening its gates for the morning market. That sun was a cold, Calvinist, invisible star unworthy of the name, its dirty gray light falling on oxcarts, countrymen laden with baskets of vegetables, women in white headdresses carrying cheeses and jugs of milk.

I was slowly making my way through the mist with my knapsacks over my shoulder, my teeth clenched to keep them from chattering. I took a quick look at the embankment of the dike where fog blended into the water and could spy nothing but vague brushstrokes of rushes, grass, and trees. It is true that for a moment I thought I glimpsed a dull reflection of metal, perhaps a morion or cuirass or even naked steel, but it was only for an instant and then the humid breath rising from the canal closed over it again. The girl walking by my side must also have seen it, because she shot me an uneasy glance from beneath the folds of the scarf that covered most of her head and face. She then turned her eyes toward the Dutch sentinels, outfitted with breastplate, helmet, and halberd, whom we could now make out—dark gray upon gray—at the outer gate of the wall, beside the drawbridge.

The city, which, in reality, was nothing more than a large town, was called Oudkerk, and it lay at the confluence of the Ooster canal, the Merck River, and the delta we Spaniards call the Mosa and the Flemish call the Maas. The city's importance was mostly military, for it controlled access to the canal along which the heretic rebels sent aid to their besieged compatriots in Breda, some three leagues away. The garrison there housed a citizen militia and two regular companies, one of them English. In addition, the fortifications were solid, and the main gate, protected by a bulwark, moat, and drawbridge, was impossible to take by ordinary means. Which was precisely why dawn found me in that place.

I suppose you may have recognized who I am. My name is Íñigo Balboa, and at the time of this tale I was fourteen years old. And may no one take it as presumption when

I tell you that he who is skillful with the dagger lives to be a veteran and that I, despite my youth, was a specialist in that art. After dangerous adventures played out in the Madrid of our king, Philip IV, in which I found myself forced to take up pistol and sword, and was once only a step away from the gallows, I had spent the last twelve months with my master, Captain Alatriste, in the Flanders army. This came about when the Tercio Viejo de Cartegna, after traveling by ship to Genoa, had come inland by way of Milan and the so-called Camino Español to join the heart of the war with the rebellious provinces. The era of glorious captains, glorious attacks, and glorious booty was now long past, and the conflict had become a kind of long and tedious chess game in which strongholds were besieged, changed hands, and then besieged again, bravery often counting for less than patience.

It was just such an episode that had brought me there that early morning walking along in the fog toward the Dutch sentinels at the Oudkerk gate as if it were something I did every day, as I and the young girl beside me, whose face was scarcely visible, the two of us surrounded by country folk, geese, oxen, and carts. We walked a little farther, even after one of the peasants, who seemed rather dark-skinned for this landscape and these people, where nearly everyone was blond, with fair skin and light eyes, passed by muttering something under his breath that sounded very much like an Ave María. He was hurrying as if he wanted to catch up with a group of four walking a little ahead of us; they, too, unusually thin and dark.

And then, at almost the same time, we all—the four in front of us, the latecomer, the girl in the scarf, and I— came together at the place where the sentinels were posted outside the drawbridge and the gate. One of the guards was a plump, pink-skinned corporal wrapped in a black cape; the other had a long blond mustache that I remember very well because he said something in Flemish, undoubtedly a lewd remark, to the young girl, and laughed aloud. And then suddenly he wasn't laughing because the thin peasant of the Ave María had pulled a dagger from his doublet and was slitting the corporal's throat. Blood spurted out in a stream so strong that it stained my knapsacks just as I was opening them to distribute the well-oiled pistols hidden inside to the four other peasants, in whose hands daggers flashed like lightning. The plump corporal opened his mouth to raise the alarm, but that was all he could do, because before he was able to utter a single syllable, a quickly drawn dagger traced a line above the neck plate of his corselet, slicing his gullet from ear to ear. By the time he had fallen into the moat, I had dropped my knapsacks and, with my own dagger between my teeth, was scrambling like a squirrel up the strut of the drawbridge. Meanwhile the girl in the scarf, who had shed her scarf and was not even a girl but a youth who answered to the name of Jaime Correas, was climbing up the other side. Like me, he shoved a wooden wedge into the mechanism of the draw-bridge and then cut its ropes and pulleys.

Oudkerk awoke as never before in its history, because the four with the pistols and he of the Ave María raced like demons along the bulwarks, stabbing and shooting any-thing that moved. At the same time, my companion and I, having put the bridge out of commission, were sliding down the chains when a hoarse roar erupted from the shore of the dike: the cries of a hundred and fifty men who had spent the night in the fog, in water up to their waists, and who now emerged shouting "Santiago! Santiago! Spain and Santiago!" the traditional battle cry in praise of their country and their patron saint. Resolved to work off the paralyzing cold with blood and fire, they swarmed up the embankment, with swords in hand, ran along the dike toward the drawbridge and the gate, occupied the bulwark, and then, to the terror of the Dutch who were scattering in all directions like crazed geese, entered the town, killing right and left.

Today the history books speak of the assault on Oudkerk as a massacre. They mention the "Spanish fury" at Antwerp, and maintain that the Tercio Viejo de Cartegna acted with singular cruelty that day. Well, no one said that to me, because I was there. It is true that those first moments were marked by pitiless carnage; but will Your Mercies tell me how else, with only a hundred and fifty men one could take a fortified Dutch town with a garrison of seven hundred? Only the horror of an unexpected and merciless attack would so quickly break the spine of those heretics, so our men applied themselves to the task with the professional rigor of experienced soldiers. The orders of Colonel don Pedro de la Daga had been to start the raid with as many deaths in order to terrify the defenders and force them to a swift surrender but not to begin the sacking of the town until victory was assured. So I will spare you further details and say only that the scene was a chaos of harquebus shot, yelling, and flashing swords and that no Dutch male over fifteen or sixteen who encountered our men in the first moments of the assault—whether fighting, fleeing, or surrendering— lived to tell of it.

Our colonel was right: The enemy's panic was our best ally, and we did not lose many men—ten or twelve, at most, counting both dead and wounded—which is, *pardiez*, few enough when compared to the two hundred heretics the town was to bury the next day and bearing in mind how smoothly Oudkerk fell into our hands. We met the strongest resistance at the city hall, where some twenty

Englishmen were able to regroup in some order. The English had been allied with the rebels ever since our lord and king had refused their Prince of Wales the hand of our Infanta María, so when the first Spaniards arrived in the town square with blood dripping from daggers, pikes, and swords, and the English welcomed them with musket volleys from the balcony of the city hall, our soldiers took it very personally. With gunpowder, tow, and tar, they set fire to the hall with the twenty Englishmen inside, then shot and knifed every one of them as they came out—those who did come out.

Then began the sacking. According to military custom, in cities that did not surrender according to the proper stipulations or that were taken by assault, the victors were entitled to enter and sack. Thus, fired with greed for booty, each soldier fought as if ten and swore for a hundred. And as Oudkerk had not surrendered—the heretic governor had been shot in the first moments and the burgomaster simultaneously hanged at the door of his house and, furthermore, as the town had been won, in a word, through pure Spanish bollocks—no one had to sign a formal order allowing us Spaniards to break into any houses we deemed promising—which was all of them—and make off with anything that took our fancy. This, as you may imagine, resulted in some painful scenes. The burghers of Flanders, like anywhere else, tended to be reluctant to be relieved of their belongings, and many had to be convinced by the tip of a sword. Soon the streets were filled with soldiers carrying a colorful variety of spoils through smoke, trampled draperies, smashed furniture, and bodies, many of which were barefoot or naked, and whose blood formed dark pools on the cobbles, blood the soldiers slipped in and the dogs lapped up. Your Mercies can imagine the picture.

There was no violation of women, at least no tolerated violation; nor was there drunkenness among the troops, for often, even in the most disciplined soldiers, the latter gives way to the former. Orders in regard to this matter were as clean-cut as the edge of a Toledo blade, for our general, don Ambrosio Spínola, did not want to antagonize the local populace still further; it was enough to be slashed and sacked without the added outrage of having their women molested. So on the eve of the attack, to make things perfectly clear—and because a lesson is always better than a lecture—two or three soldiers who had been convicted for crimes against the gentle sex were hanged. No unit and no company is perfect. Even in Christ's, which was one he had recruited himself, there was one who betrayed him, another who denied him, and yet another who failed to believe him. The fact is that in Oudkerk, the preventative warning worked wonders, and except for an occasional isolated case, inevitable when dealing with soldiers drunk with victory and booty, the virtue of the Flemish women, whatever it may have been, remained intact. For the moment.

The city hall burned right down until there was nothing left but the weathervane. I was with Jaime Correas, both of us happy that we had saved our hides at the gate of the bulwark and that we had carried out our assigned mission to the satisfaction of all, except, of course, the Dutch. In my knapsacks, recovered after the fight and still stained with the blood of the Dutchman with the blond mustache, we stowed everything of value we could find: silver cutlery, a few gold coins, a gold chain we had taken from the corpse of a burgher, and a new and magnificent pair of pewter jugs. My companion had donned a handsome plumed morion that had belonged to an Englishman who no longer had a head on which to display it, and I was strutting around in a fine silver-trimmed red velvet doublet I'd found in an abandoned house we had ransacked at our pleasure.

Jaime, like me, was a *mochilero*, that is, a lowly aide or soldier's page, and together we had lived through enough exhaustion and hardship to think of ourselves as good comrades. For Jaime, the booty and the success of events at the drawbridge, which don Carmelo Bragado, the captain of our company, had promised to reward if all went well, was consolation for having been disguised as a girl;

we had drawn lots for that, but it had nonetheless left him somewhat embarrassed. As for me, by this point in my Flanders adventure I had decided that I wanted to be a soldier when I reached the required age, and all the excitement had induced a kind of vertigo, a youthful intoxication tasting of gunpowder, glory, and exaltation. That is how, 'fore God, a lad the same age as the number of lines in a sonnet comes to witness a war when the goddess Fortuna decrees that he will not play the part of victim but of witness and, at times, of precocious executioner. But I have already told Your Mercies, on a different occasion, that those were times when a life, even one's own, was worth less than the steel used to take it. Difficult and cruel times. Hard times.

I was telling you that we had reached the square of the city hall, and we stayed there awhile, fascinated by the fire and the dead Englishmen, many of whom were blond or red-haired and freckled, piled up naked by the doors. From time to time we came across Spaniards laden with booty or groups of terrified Hollanders watching from the columns of the square, huddled together like sheep under the watchful eyes of our comrades, who were armed to the teeth. We went over to take a look. There were women, old men, and children but few adult males. I recall a youth about our age who looked at us with an expression somewhere between sullen and curious, and blond, pale-skinned women who stood wide-eyed beneath their white headdresses, their blue, fearful eyes observing our dark-haired soldiers. Our men were not as tall as the Flemish men, but they had full mustaches, heavy beards, and strong legs. Each had a musket over his shoulder and a sword in his hand, and each was clad in leather and metal stained with grime, blood, gun powder, and mud from the dike. I will never forget the way those people looked at us Spaniards, there in Oudkerk as in so many other places: the blend of hatred and fear when they saw us enter their cities and march past their houses, covered with the dust of the road, bristling with iron, and ragged as urchins, boisterous at times but more dangerous when not. Proud, even in misery, as Bartolomé Torres Naharro wrote in his *Soldadesca*.

In war, come what may,
there is this much I can say,
if a man has two hands
gold will surely roll his way.

We were the loyal infantry of the Catholic king: volunteers, all of us, in search of fortune or glory; men of honor but often also the dregs of the Spanish empire; rabble given to mutiny, who demonstrated flawless iron discipline but only when facing enemy fire. Dauntless and terrible even in defeat, the Spanish *tercios,* a training school for the best soldiers Europe had produced in two centuries, comprised the most efficient military machine anyone had ever commanded on a field of battle. Although at that time, with the age of the great assaults over and with artillery taking the fore, the war in Flanders had become one long succession of sieges, of mines and trenches, and our infantry was no longer the splendid military force our great Philip II had put his faith in when he wrote his famous letter to his ambassador to the Pope:

I do not plan, nor do I wish to be the lord of heretics. Yet if the situation cannot be remedied as I would have it, without resorting to weapons, then I am determined to take them up, and neither the danger in which I place myself nor the ruin of those lands nor of the rest of those still mine, can prevent me from doing what a Christian, God-fearing prince must do in His service.

And that, *pardiez,* is how it was. After long decades of crossing swords with half the world without achieving much more than icy feet and hot heads, very soon there would be nothing left for Spain than to watch her *tercios* die on fields of battle like the one at Rocroi, faithful to their reputation—lacking anything else—taciturn and impassive when their lines formed into those "human towers and walls" the Frenchman Bossuet wrote of with such admiration. But yes, there is this: We fucked them good and hard. Even though our men and their generals were no equal to those in the days of the Duque de Alba and Alejandro Farnesio, Spanish soldiers continued to be Europe's nightmare for some time: they who had captured a French king in Pavía, triumphed in San Quintín, sacked Rome and Antwerp, taken Amiens and Ostende, killed ten thousand enemies in the attack on Jemmigen, eight thousand in Maastrich, and nine thousand in Sluys, wielding steel in water up to their waists. We were the very wrath of God, and it took only one glance at us to understand why: We were a rough and rowdy horde from the dry lands of the south, fighting in hostile foreign lands where there was no possible retreat and defeat meant annihilation. Driven men, some by the poverty and hunger they meant to leave behind and others by ambition for land, fortune and glory, to whom the song of the gentle youth in *Don Quijote* might apply:

It is necessity that
carries me to war;
for had I money,
I would ne'er have come this far.

And those other old and eloquent lines:

I do battle out of need,
and once seated in the saddle,
Castile grows ever vaster
beneath the hoof beats of my steed.

So. The fact is that we were still there and would continue thus for several years more, enlarging Castile with
the blades of our swords or as God and the devil had taught
us in Oudkerk. The banner of our company was flying
from the balcony of a house in the square, and my comrade, Jaime Correas, who was a *mochilero* in the squad of
Second Lieutenant Coto, went there to look for his people.
I went on a bit farther, past the front of the city hall to escape the terrible heat of the fire, and as I rounded the
building I saw two individuals piling up the books and documents they were carrying out of the door as fast as they
could. What they were doing did not appear to be
pillaging—it would be rare in the midst of widespread
sacking for anyone to bother about books—but instead they
seemed to be rescuing what they could from the fire.
I went to take a closer look. Your Mercies may recall that
I had some experience of the written word from my days
in la Villa y Corte de las Españas that is, Madrid, owing to
my friendship with don Francisco de Quevedo, who had

given me Plutarch to read; Dómine Pérez's lessons in Latin and grammar; my taste for Lope's theater; and my master Captain Alatriste's habit of reading wherever there was a book to be read.

One of the men carrying books out and piling them in the street was an elderly Dutchman with long white hair. He was wearing black, as pastors there did, with a dirty collar and gray hose. He did not, however, appear to be a religious man, if one may call those who preach the doctrines of that heretic Calvin religious—may lightning strike the whoreson in hell or wherever he may be stewing. In the end, I took him to be a secretary or city official trying to rescue books from the conflagration. I would have passed right by had I not noticed that the other individual, staggering through the smoke with his arms filled with books, wore the red band of the Spanish soldiers. He was a young man, bareheaded, and his face was covered with sweat and soot, as if he had already made many trips into the depths of the blazing inferno the building had become. A sword swung from his baldric and he was wearing high boots blackened from charred wood and debris. He seemed to give little importance to the smoking sleeve of his doublet, not even when, finally noticing it as he set his load of books on the ground, he put it out with a couple of distracted swipes. At that moment he looked up and saw me. He had a thin, angular face and a trim chestnut-brown mustache that flowed into a short pear-shaped beard beneath his lower lip. I judged him to be between twenty to twenty-five years old.

"You could give me a hand," he grunted, when he noticed the faded *aspa*, the red Saint Andrew's cross, I wore sewn to my doublet, "instead of standing there gawking."

He glanced toward the columns of the square, where a few women and children were taking in the scene, and wiped the sweat from his face with the singed sleeve.

"God help me," he said, "but I am burning with thirst."

He turned and accompanied by the fellow in black, ran back to search for more books. After considering the situation for an instant, I raced to the nearest house, where a frightened Dutch family was watching with curiosity in front of a door that had been battered off its hinges.

"Drinken," I said, holding out my two pewter jugs. I pantomimed drinking and then clapped one hand to the hilt of my dagger. The Dutch understood both word and gesture, for they filled the jugs with water, and I returned to where the two men were stacking books from another foray. When they saw the jugs, they dispatched the contents without taking a breath. Before plunging once more into the smoke, the Spaniard turned to me.

"Thank you," he said very simply.

I followed him. I set my knapsacks on the ground and took off my velvet doublet, not because as he thanked me he had smiled nor because I was touched by his singed sleeve and his smoke-reddened eyes but because suddenly that anonymous soldier had made me realize that at times there are more important things than collecting booty, even if the latter can sometimes be worth a hundred times one's yearly pay. So I took as deep a breath as I could, and, covering my mouth and nose with a handkerchief I extracted from my pouch, I ducked my head to avoid the sputtering beams that were threatening to collapse and ran blindly into the smoke. I pulled books from the flaming shelves until the heat became asphyxiating and the embers floating in the air burned my throat with every breath. Most of the books were ashes by now, dust that was not "enamored," as it was in that beautiful and distant sonnet by don Francisco de Quevedo, but only a sad residue, all the hours of study, all the love, all the intelligence, all the lives that could have illuminated other lives now vanished.

We made our last trip before the ceiling of the library collapsed in an explosion of flames that roared at our backs. Outside, we stood gasping for air, stupefied, clammy with sweat, our eyes tearing from the smoke. At our feet were around two hundred books and old documents. A tenth, I calculated, of what had burned inside the library. On his knees beside the pile, drained by his efforts, the Dutchman in black coughed and wept. When he had caught his breath, the soldier smiled at me as he had when I brought the water.

"What is your name, lad?"

I stood a little straighter, swallowing my last cough.

"Íñigo Balboa," I said. "From the *bandera* of Captain don Carmelo Bragado."

That was not strictly accurate. It was true that the *bandera* was indeed the one Diego Alatriste fought with and therefore mine, but in the *tercios* a *mochilero* was considered little more than a servant or bearer, not a soldier. But that did not seem to matter to the stranger.

"Thank you, Íñigo Balboa," he said.

His smile widened, lighting up a face gleaming with sweat and black with smoke.

"Some day," he added, "you will remember what you did today."

A curious thing, by my faith. He had no way to divine it, but, as Your Mercies witness, it was true what that soldier said. I do remember very well. He put one hand on my shoulder and grasped one of my hands with the other. His was a strong, warm clasp. And then, without exchanging a word with the Dutchman stacking books in piles as if they were a precious treasure (and now I know that they were), he turned and walked away.

Several years would go by before I again encountered the anonymous soldier I had helped one foggy autumn day during the sacking of Oudkerk. In all that time I had never learned his name. It was only later, when I was a grown man, that I had the good fortune to meet him again, in Madrid and in circumstances that have nothing to do with the thread of the present tale. By then he was no longer an obscure soldier, and, despite the years that had passed since that morning long ago, he still remembered my name. And I at last would know his: He was Pedro Calderón, the famous playwright Pedro Calderón de la Barca, known throughout Spain.

But let us return to Oudkerk. After the soldier and I left the square, I went in search of Captain Alatriste, whom I found in good health, along with the rest of his squad. They were gathered around a small bonfire in the rear garden of a house that backed onto the dock of the canal, near the city wall. The captain and his comrades had been ordered to attack that section of the town, burn the ships at the docks, and secure the rear gate, thereby cutting off the retreat of enemy troops. When I caught up with the captain, the charred remains of burned ships were smoldering along the shore, and traces of the recent battle were visible on the dock, in the gardens, and in the houses.

"Íñigo," said the captain.

His smile was weary and a little distant, and he had that look that remains imprinted on soldiers following a difficult battle, a look that the veterans of the *tercios* called "the last stand," a look that during the time I had spent in Flanders I had learned to distinguish from other looks, such as that of weariness, resignation, fear, and absolute resolve. This was the look that stays in the eyes after other emotions have passed through them, the precise expression Captain Alatriste's face wore at that moment. He was sitting on a bench, his elbow on the table by his side, his left leg extended as if it pained him. His knee-high boots were covered with mud, and he was wearing a dirty brown-sleeved doublet; it was unbuttoned, allowing me a glimpse of his usual buffcoat beneath it. His hat lay on the table beside a pistol—I could see it had been fired—and his belt with his sword and dagger.

"Come over to the fire."

Gratefully, I obeyed, as I took in the corpses of three Dutchmen lying close by: one on the planking of the nearby dock, another beneath the table. The third Dutchman was sprawled face down at the threshold of the back door of the house and held a halberd that had not served to save his life—or anything else for that matter. I observed that his pockets had been turned inside out, his corselet and shoes had been removed, and two fingers of one hand were missing, doubtless because whoever had taken his rings had been in a hurry. A brownish-red trail of blood led across the garden to the spot where the captain was sitting.

"That one won't feel the cold any longer," said one of the soldiers.

From the strong accent I did not need to turn to turn around to know that the person who had spoken was Mendieta, a Basque like myself, a thick-browed, burly man from Biscay whose mustache was almost as impressive as my master's. The little troupe was completed by Curro Garrote, a Malagüeno from Los Percheles, so tanned he looked like a Moor; the Mallorcan José Llop, and Sebastián Copons, an old comrade of Captain Alatriste from earlier campaigns. Copons was a dried-up little man from Aragon as tough as the mother who gave him birth, and his face might had been carved from the stone of Mallos de Riglos. Sitting nearby were three others from the squad: the Olivares brothers and the Galician, Rivas.

All of them knew of my difficult assignment at the drawbridge and were happy to see me alive and well, though they did not make any great show of it. For one thing, it was not the first time I had smelled powder in Flanders, and, besides, they had their own affairs to think about. Beyond that, they were not the kind of soldier who makes a fuss over something that was, in truth, considered the duty of anyone in the pay of our king. Although in our case—or, rather in theirs, for we *mochileros* did not have the right to claim benefits or wages—the *tercio* had gone a long time without seeing the color of a piece of eight.

Nor did Diego Alatriste outdo himself in his welcome. I have already said that he limited his greeting to a slight smile, twisting his mustache as if he were thinking about something else. But when he saw that I was hanging around like a good dog hoping to be petted by its master, he complimented my red velvet doublet and in the end offered me a hunk of bread and some sausages his companions were roasting over the fire. Their clothing was still wet after the night spent in the waters of the canal, and their faces, dirty and greasy from their vigil and the subsequent battle, reflected their exhaustion. They were nonetheless in good humor. They were alive, everything had gone well, the town was again Catholic and subject to our lord and king, and the booty—several sacks and knotted cloths piled in a corner—was reasonable.

"After a three months' fast from pay," commented Curro Garrote, cleaning the bloody rings of the dead Dutchman, "this is a reprieve."

From the other side of the town came the sound of bugles and drums. The fog was beginning to lift, and that allowed us to see a thin line of soldiers moving along the Ooster dike. The long pikes advancing through the last remnants of gray fog resembled a field of swaying reeds, and a short-lived ray of sun, sent ahead as if it were a scout, glinted off the metal of their lances, morions, and corselets and reproduced them in the quiet waters of the canal.

At their head came horses and banners bearing the good and ancient cross of Saint Andrew, or of Burgundy: the red *aspa* insignia of the Spanish *tercios*.

"Here comes Jiñalasoga," said Garrote. Jiñalasoga was the nickname the veterans had given don Pedro de la Daga, colonel of the Viejo Tercio de Cartagena. In the soldier's tongue of the time, *jiñar* meant—begging your pardon, Your Mercies—"to empty your bowels," that is, "to shit." This may sound a little common, here in this tale, but, *pardiez*, we were soldiers, not San Plácido nuns. As for the *soga* part, no one who knew our colonel's taste for hanging his men for disciplinary offences could harbor any doubt regarding the appropriateness of "rope" in his sobriquet. The fact is that Jiñalasoga, more formally, colonel don Pedro de la Daga—either will do—was commanding the relief forces of Captain don Hernán Torralba and was coming along the dike to take official possession of Oudkerk.

"He gets here midmorning," grumbled Mendieta, "after all the slashing's been done."

Diego Alatriste slowly got to his feet; I saw that he did so with difficulty and that the leg he had stretched before him was giving him constant pain. I knew that this was not a new wound but, rather, a year-old injury to his hip he'd received in the alleyways near the Plaza Mayor in Madrid at the time of his next-to-last encounter with his old enemy, Gualterio Malatesta. Dampness precipitated a rheumatic pain, and the night spent in the waters of the Ooster was no prescription for a cure.

"Let's go take a look."

He smoothed his mustache, buckled on the belt that held his sword and *vizcaína* dagger, thrust his pistol into his waistband, and picked up the wide-brimmed hat with the perennially frowsy red plume. Then slowly, very slowly, he turned to Mendieta.

"Colonels always arrive midmorning," he said, and from his cold, gray-green eyes it was impossible to know whether he was speaking seriously or in jest. "Which is why we ourselves must get up so early."

2. THE DUTCH WINTER

Weeks went by, then months, and we were well into winter. And although our general don Ambrosio Spínola had the rebellious provinces on the rack again, we were losing Flanders; bit by bit it slipped away, until finally we lost it completely. If you will, Your Mercies, consider very carefully that when I say Flanders was slipping away, I mean that only the powerful Spanish military machine maintained the gradually weakening link to those distant lands from which a letter—even by the fastest post horses—took three weeks to reach Madrid. To the north the Estates General, backed by France, England, Venice, and the other enemies of Spain, were being strengthened in their rebellion thanks to the cult of Calvinism, which was more useful in the business dealings of their burghers and merchants than the oppressive, antiquated *true* religion, which seemed so impractical to those who preferred to deal with a God who applauded revenue, and were shaking off the yoke of a too distant centralist and authoritarian Castilian monarchy. For their part, the Catholic states of the south, though still loyal, were beginning to grow weary both of the cost of a war that had been going on for eighty years and of the excessive demands and damage done by soldiers who were increasingly thought of as occupying troops. All these things were poisoning the air, and to that we must add the decadence of Spain itself, in which a well-intentioned but ineffective king, an intelligent but overly ambitious prime minister, a sterile aristocracy, a corrupt officialdom, and a clergy as stupid as it was fanatic, were hurtling us headfirst into the abyss. Catalonia and Portugal were on the point of withdrawing from the crown; the latter, forever.

Stultified among kings, aristocrats, and priests, with church and civil traditions that diminished those who tried to earn an honorable living with their hands, we Spaniards preferred to seek our fortune by fighting in Flanders or conquering America, pursuing the stroke of luck that would allow us to live like lords without paying taxes or lifting a finger. That was what caused our looms and lathes to fall silent, what depopulated and impoverished Spain, and what reduced us first to a legion of adventurers, then to a people of mendicant hidalgos, and finally to a rabble of base Sancho Panzas. And that was also how the vast heritage bequeathed to our lord and king by his grandfathers, that Spain upon which the sun never set—for when that star sank below one of her horizons it rose upon another—continued to be what she was, thanks only to the gold the galleons brought from the Indies, and the pikes—the famous lances Diego Velázquez would very soon immortalize—of the veteran armies. For those reasons, despite our decadence, we were not yet disdained and were even still feared. So it was timely and just—as well as a slap in the face to other nations—that one could say:

Who spoke here of war?
Is our memory still clear?
When the name Castile is spoken
does the earth still shake with fear?

I hope that Your Mercies will make allowances when I so immodestly include myself in this panorama, but at that point in the Flanders campaign, that very young Íñigo Balboa you knew during the adventure of the two Englishmen and later in the incident at the convent, was no longer quite so young. The winter of '24, which the Viejo Tercio de Cartegena spent garrisoned in Oudkerk, found me in the full vigor of my youth. I have already said that the smell of gunpowder was nothing new to me, and although

I could not, because of my age, carry a pike, sword, or harquebus in combat, my status as the *mochilero* of the squad in which Captain Alatriste served had made me a veteran of every imaginable adventure. My instincts were already those of a soldier: I could smell a lighted harquebus cord half a league away, I knew the pounds and ounces of every cannon ball or musket shot by the sound, and I was developing a singular talent in the task we *mochileros* called foraging: incursions into surrounding territory, scavenging for firewood and food. Our raids were indispensable when, as now, the land had been devastated by war, supplies were short, and everyone had to scramble for himself. Ours was not an easy task, and the proof is that in Amiens, the French and English had killed some eighty *mochileros*, some only twelve years old, as they foraged through the countryside—inhuman butchery, even in time of war—which the Spaniards appropriately avenged by knifing two hundred of Albion's soldiers, because those who dole it out must also be able take it. And if in the long run the subjects of the queens and kings of England beleaguered us in many campaigns, it is fair to record that we, in turn, dispatched not a few, and that, without being as robust as they or as blond or as loud-mouthed when drinking beer, when it came to arrogance, no one ever put us in the shade. Besides, if the Englishman fought with the courage of national pride, we did so out of

national desperation, which was not—no definitely not—
chickenfeed. So, we made them pay with their accursed
hides, theirs, and so many others.

Well, this was just—it's nothing really—
a leg I lost, blown off by a volley.
What can those Lutheran dogs be thinking,
to take my legs but leave me my hands.

In short: During that winter of wavering light, fog,
and gray rain, I foraged and pillaged and scavenged from
one end of that Flemish land to the other. It was not arid
like the greater part of Spain—God did not smile upon us
even in that—but nearly all green, like the fields of my
native Oñate, though much flatter and scored with rivers
and canals. In such activities—stealing hens, digging
turnips, holding my dagger to the throat of peasants as
hungry as I and taking their meager store of food—
I revealed myself to be a consummate specialist. I did,
and would in years to come, many things I am not proud
to remember; but I survived the winter, I aided my
comrades, and I became a man in all the disparate and
terrible meanings of the word.

To serve my king, I took up the sword
'ere downy fuzz covered my lip.

Words Lope wrote about himself. I also lost my virginity, or my virtue, which is the way the good Dómine Pérez put it. For at that point, in Flanders, half-lad and half-soldier, that was one of the few things I had left to lose. But that is a very personal and intimate story, and I have no intention of detailing it here for Your Mercies.

Diego Alatriste's squad was the principal unit fighting under the banner of Captain don Carmelo Bragado, and it was formed only of the best: not a lily-livered man among them, only soldiers quick with a sword and born to suffer and to fight. All of them were veterans who had under their belts at least the Palatinate campaign or years of service in the Mediterranean with the *tercios* of Naples or Sicily, which was the case of the Malagüeño Curro Garrote. Others, like the Mallorcan José Llop or the Basque Mendieta, had fought in Flanders, before the Twelve Years' truce, and the yellowed service records of a few, like Copons, who was from Huesca, and like Alatriste himself, went back as far as the last years of our good Philip II, may God hold that good king in glory. It was under Philip's old banners that—as Lope would say—the swords and beards of those two had appeared simultaneously.

Taking losses and additions into account, the squad usually numbered between ten and fifteen men, depending on the situation, and it had no specific function in the company other than to move quickly and back up others in their various actions, carrying half a dozen harquebuses and about as many muskets. The squad operated in a unique way: It had no *cabo*, the leader appointed by the captain, for in any engagement they were under the direct orders of Captain Bragado himself, who might use them in the line with others from the unit or give them a free hand in surprise attacks, scouting missions, skirmishes, and raids. They were all, as I said, conditioned to gunfire and expert in their responsibilities, and it was perhaps for that reason that in their operations—even without having identified a leader or acting under a formal hierarchy of any sort—they had, in a kind of tacit accord, bestowed authority on Diego Alatriste.

As for the three *escudos* that went along with being head of the squad, it was Captain Bragado who collected them, in addition to the wages of forty *escudos* due as actual captain of the unit, since that was how he was listed in the documents of the *tercio*. Although he was a man of stature, owing to his family background, and a reasonable officer as long as his discipline was not questioned, don Carmelo Bragado was one of those men who hears *clink* and says *mine*. He never let so much as a *maravedí* get past him, and even went so far as to keep dead and deserters on the rolls in order to collect their pay . . . when there was pay.

However, I have to say that it was a widespread practice, and in Bragado's favor we can say two things: He never refused to help soldiers in need, and he personally had twice proposed Diego Alatriste's promotion to squad leader, though both times Alatriste had declined.

As to the esteem in which Bragado held my master, I need say only that four years earlier at White Mountain, when General Tilly's first assault and second attack under the orders of Count Bouquoy and Colonel don Guillermo Verdugo failed, Alatriste and Captain Bragado (and Lope Balboa, my father, right along with them) had climbed shoulder to shoulder up the slopes, fighting for every foot of corpse-strewn terrain. Then a year after that, on the plains of Fleurus, when don Gonzalo de Córdoba won the battle but the Cartagena *tercio* was nearly annihilated after holding fast against several cavalry charges, Diego Alatriste was among the last of the dauntless Spaniards who never broke ranks around the flag that, with the standard bearer dead, along with all the other officers, was held high by Captain Bragado himself. And, *pardiez*, in that time, and among those men, such things still counted for something.

It was raining in Flanders. 'Pon my word, it rained pitchforks and anvils that accursed autumn and through that whole accursed winter, turning to pure mud the flat, shifting, swampy land that was crossed in every direction by rivers, canals, and dikes that seemed to have been laid out by the hand of the devil himself. It rained for days, for weeks, for months, until the gray landscape of low clouds was completely erased. It was a strange land with an unfamiliar tongue, populated by people who despised and at the same time feared us; a countryside denuded by the season and the war, lacking any defense against the cold, the wind, and the water. There were no peaches in that land, or figs, or cherries, or peppers, or saffron, or olives, or oil, or oranges, or rosemary, or pines, or laurels, or cypresses. There was not even any sun, only a tepid disk that moved indolently behind a veil of clouds. The place our iron-and-leather-clad men had come from, men who plodded on though their bodies yearned for the clear skies of the south, was far away, as far as the ends of the earth. And those rough, proud soldiers now in the lands of the north repaying the courtesy of a visit received centuries before at the fall of the Roman empire, recognized that they were very few in number and a great distance from any friendly country.

Niccolo Machiavelli had already written that the courage of our infantry grew out of necessity. As the Florentine writer acknowledged, quite against his pleasure, for he could never bear the Spanish, "Fighting in a strange land, and seeing themselves, absent the possibility of flee-

ing, forced to die or conquer, makes them very good soldiers." Applied to Flanders, that is absolutely true: there
were never more than twenty thousand Spaniards in that
land and never more than eight thousand together in one
place. But that was the impetus that allowed us to be masters of Europe for a century and a half: knowing that only
victories kept us safe among hostile peoples and that if
defeated we had nowhere we could reach on foot. That was
why we fought to the end with the cruelty of our ancestors,
the courage of men who expect nothing, the religious
fanaticism and insolence that one of our captains, don
Diego de Acuña, expressed better than anyone in his
famous, passionate, and truculent toast:

To Spain; and may he who wishes
to defend her die an honorable death,
and may he who is traitor to her
be dishonored to his last breath;
may no cross mark his remains,
may his burial ground remain unblessed,
and may he lack a loyal son
to close his eyes in Christian rest.

As I was telling Your Mercies, the morning that Captain
Bragado made an inspection visit to the advanced posts
where his *bandera* was quartered, it was raining down in
buckets. The captain was from León, in the Bierzo district.

He was a large man, about six feet tall, and to get him through the mud and mire he had somewhere requisitioned a Dutch workhorse, a large animal with strong legs appropriate for its burden. Diego Alatriste was leaning against the window, watching the rivulets of rain sliding down the thick glass panes, when he saw his captain coming along the dike on horseback, his sodden hat brim drooping from the unceasing rain and a waxed cape over his shoulders.

"Warm a little wine," Alatriste said to the woman at his back.

He said it in an elementary Flemish—*verwarm wijn* were his words—then continued to watch through the window as the woman poked the miserable peat fire, then set atop the stove a tin jug she took from the table where a few bread crusts and boiled cabbage were being dispatched by Copons, Mendieta, and the others. Everything looked dirty. Soot from the stove had blackened the wall and the ceiling, and the smell of bodies too long enclosed within the four walls of the house and the odor of dampness filtering through the beams and roof tiles could have been cut with any of the daggers or swords scattered around the room among harquebuses, goatskin buffcoats, heavy outdoor gear, and dirty clothing. It smelled of barracks, of winter, and of misery. It smelled of soldiers and of Flanders.

The grayish light sifting through the window accentuated the scars and hollows on Diego Alatriste's unshaven face, making the fixed clarity of his eyes even colder. He was in his shirtsleeves, with his doublet thrown over his shoulders and two harquebus cords knotted below his knees to hold up the legs of his cobbled leather boots. Without moving from the window, he watched as Captain Bragado got off his horse, pushed open the door, and then, shaking the water from his hat and cape, came inside with a pair of oaths and a "By the good Christ," cursing the rain, the mud, and all of Flanders.

"Go on eating, men," he said, "since you have something to eat."

The soldiers, who had half-risen, went back to their meager rations, and Bragado, whose clothing began to steam as he neared the stove, accepted the piece of hard bread and bowl with the last of the cabbage offered him by Mendieta. The captain studied the woman closely as he accepted the jar of warm wine she put into his hands, and after warming his fingers on the metal, he drank with short sips, casting sideways glances at the man who had not moved from the window.

"By God, Capitán Alatriste," he ventured after a bit. "You are not badly quartered here."

It was extraordinary to hear the captain of the unit address Diego Alatriste as *Capitán* so naturally, which proves to what point Alatriste and his honorary rank were known to all and respected even by his superiors. As Carmelo Bragado spoke, he turned covetous eyes toward the woman, who was some thirty years old and blonde like nearly all the women of her land. She was not particularly pretty: Her hands were reddened by work and her teeth were uneven, but she had fair skin, broad hips beneath her skirts, and full breasts that threatened to overflow the bodice tightly laced in the style of the women painted in that era by Peter Paul Rubens. In sum, she had the look of a healthy goose that Flemish countrywomen tend to have when they are not overly ripe. And all this—as Captain Bragado and even the most dimwitted recruit could have divined merely by observing the way the girl and Diego Alatriste ignored each other in public—was much to the displeasure of her husband, a well-off, fiftyish peasant with a sour face. He roamed about, forcing himself to be subservient to the feared, gruff foreigners he hated with all his soul but that fortune had sent him with a billeting warrant. A husband who had no choice but to swallow his anger and despair each night when after hearing his wife slip silently from his side, he listened to the barely muffled moans in the crunching corn-husk pallet where Alatriste slept. How that had come about is something that belongs to the private life of the couple. In any case, the husband received certain advantages in exchange: His house, his property, and his neck were saved, something that could not be said in every place Spaniards were quartered. Cuckolded he may have been, but at least his wife was sneaking off to one man, and one of high rank at that, and not to several, or by force. After all, in Flanders, as in any place and any time of war, a man who does not find ways to console himself is miserably discontented. The greatest solace for nearly everyone was surviving, and that husband, whatever else, was alive.

"I bring orders," Captain Bragado said, "for an incursion along the Geertrudeidenberg road. Without too much killing. Only to pry loose a little information."

"Prisoners?" asked Alatriste.

"Two or three would not go amiss. Apparently our General Spínola believes that the Dutch are preparing to send help to Breda by boat, taking advantage of the rising waters from the rains. It would be helpful if a few men went a league in that direction to confirm the rumor. Done quietly, of course. Discreetly."

Quietly or with bugles blaring, a league through that rain and the mud of the roads was asking a lot, but none of the men showed any surprise. They knew that the same rain kept the Dutch in their bunkers and trenches and that they would be snoring like pigs while a handful of Spaniards slipped by beneath their noses.

Diego Alatriste stroked his mustache. "When do we leave?"

"Now."

"Number of men?"

"The whole squad."

That brought a curse from one of the men at the table, and Captain Bragado whirled around, eyes shooting sparks. All heads were lowered, all eyes cast down. Alatriste, who had recognized the voice of Curro Garrote, sent the Malagüeño a reproachful look.

"Perhaps," Bragado said very slowly, "one of these soldiers has something to say on the subject."

He had set the jar of wine down on the table without finishing it and had placed his hand to the hilt of his sword. His strong yellow teeth were gritted beneath his mustache. The effect was extremely disagreeable: They looked like the teeth of a bulldog ready to attack.

"No one has anything to say," Alatriste replied.

"Better so."

Garrote had looked up, piqued by that "no one." He was a thin, dark-skinned rough-and-tumble type with a sparse beard that curled like those of the Turks he had fought against while in the galleys of Naples and Sicily. His hair was long and greasy, and he wore a gold earring in his left ear. There was none in the right because, according to him, a Turk's scimitar had sliced off the lobe while Garrote was on the island of Cyprus, though others attributed the loss to a certain knife fight in a whorehouse in Ragusa.

"But," he broke in, "I do have something to say to señor Capitán Bragado. Three things. One is that it is all the same to the son of my mother whether we walk two leagues in the rain with Hollanders, with Turks, or with their whoring mothers . . . "

He spoke firmly, adamantly, verging on impertinence, and his companions watched with expectation, some with visible approval. They were all veterans, and obedience to the military hierarchy was natural, but so was arrogance, for their status as soldiers also made them all hidalgos. The tradition of discipline, the bone and sinew of the old *tercios*, had been recognized even by an Englishman, a certain Gascoigne, when writing about the Spanish Fury and his account of the sacking of Antwerp. He had said, "The Walloons and the Germans are as undisciplined as the Spanish are admirable for their discipline." Which is no small recognition from an English author when he is speaking of Spaniards. As for arrogance, it is not wasted time to recount the opinion of don Francisco de Valdez, who had been a captain, a sergeant-major, and then a colonel, and who therefore knew a spade for a spade, when he affirmed in his *Espejo y disciplina militar* that "Nearly always they abhor to be bound to order, particularly the Spanish infantryman, who, being more choleric than others, has little patience." These men were nothing like the deliberate and phlegmatic Flemish, who, though avaricious in the extreme, did not lie or fly into a rage but proceeded with great calm. The courage and fortitude of the Spaniards in Flanders, which along with their conduct in adversity forged the miracle of iron discipline on the field of battle, also made them less than gentle in other circumstances, such as dealing with their superiors, who had to move cautiously and with great tact. It was not a rare occurrence, despite the threat of the gallows, for a simple soldier to knife a sergeant or a captain over real or supposed offenses, embarrassing punishment, even a word out of place.

Knowing all this, Bragado turned to Diego Alatriste, as if to ask, wordlessly, his judgment of the situation, but he was met only with an impassive face. Alatriste was a person who let each man assume responsibility for what he said and what he did.

"You spoke of three things," said Bragado, turning again to Garrote with a great amount of calm but even more menacing sangfroid. "What are the other two?"

"It has been a long time since any cloth has come our way, and we are wearing rags," the Malagüeño continued, entirely unintimidated. "No provender reaches us, and since sacking is forbidden, we are reduced to near starvation. These vile Hollanders hide their best victuals, and when they don't, they ask for gold in exchange." He pointed with rancor toward their host, who was watching from the other room. "I am sure that if we could tickle his ribs with a dagger, that dog would somehow discover a full pantry or a buried pot filled with nice, shiny florins."

Captain Bragado was listening patiently; he still appeared to be calm but had not taken his hand from the hilt of his Toledo steel.

"And the third?"

Garrote raised his tone slightly, just enough to express arrogance without overdoing it. He knew that Bragado was not a man to tolerate a word meant to best him, not from his veteran soldiers . . . not even from the pope. But from the king? Well, he had no choice but to accept that.

"The third and principal item, Capitán, is that these good soldiers, who with good reason you address as Your Mercies, have not collected pay in five months."

This time quiet murmurs of agreement ran around the table. Only the Aragonese Copons said nothing; he was staring at the crust of bread he had been crumbling into his bowl and then scooping out with his fingers. The captain turned to Diego Alatriste, still at his place by the window. Alatriste's lips did not move, and he held Bragado's gaze.

"And do you stand by that, Capitan?" Bragado asked him gruffly.

Alatriste shrugged his shoulders, his expression inscrutable. "I stand by what I say," he stated. "And at times

I stand by what my comrades do, but at the moment, I have said nothing, and they have done nothing."

"But this soldier has gifted us with his opinion."

"Opinions belong to those who hold them."

"And that is why you have nothing to say and why you are looking at me in that way, señor Alatriste?"

"That is why I have nothing to say and why, Capitán, I am looking at you."

Bragado studied him carefully and then slowly acquiesced. The two knew each other well, and in addition, the officer had good judgment when it came to distinguishing between firmness and affront. After a moment he withdrew his hand from his sword and touched his chin, but as he glanced at the men around the table, the hand returned to the hilt of his sword.

"No one has collected his pay," he said finally, and he seemed to be speaking to Alatriste, as if it had been he and not Garrote who had spoken, as if he were the one who merited an answer. "Not Your Mercies, nor I myself. Not our colonel, nor even General Spínola. Withal that don Ambrosio is Genoese and from a family of bankers!"

Diego Alatriste listened in silence and said nothing. His gray-green eyes were still locked with those of the officer. Bragado had not served in Flanders before the Twelve Year's Truce, but Alatriste had, and during that time mutinies had been the order of the day. Both knew that Alatriste had more than once experienced mutiny at close hand, when the troops had refused to fight after months, even years, of not collecting their wages. He had never, however, counted himself among the insurgents, not even when the precarious financial situation of Spain had institutionalized mutiny as the one means by which troops obtained their due. The other alternative was sacking, as in Rome and Antwerp:

I have come here without food
but should I request a morsel
I am shown a thousand Dutchmen
and an impregnable castle.

Nonetheless, in that campaign, except in the case of places taken by attack or in the heat of action, it had been General Spínola's policy not to inflict excessive violence upon the civilian population, so as not to exacerbate their already exhausted sympathies. Breda, should it fall, would not be sacked, and the fatigue of those who besieged it would not be rewarded. Therefore, facing the prospect of no booty and no pay, the soldiers were beginning to wear long faces and to huddle in corners and whisper. Even a dolt could read the signs.

"Furthermore, as far as I am aware," Bragado continued, "only soldiers of other nations claim their pay *before* they fight."

That, too, was very true. With no money to be had, reputation was all we had left, and it is well known that within the Spanish *tercios* it was a point of honor neither to demand back pay nor to mutiny before a battle, so that no one could say we had acted out of fear. Even on the dunes of Nieuport and in Alost, troops who were already rebelling suspended their demands and charged into combat. Unlike the Swiss, Italians, English, and Germans, who often asked for unpaid wages as a condition for their service, Spanish soldiers mutinied only after victory.

"I believed," was Bragado's last comment, "that I was dealing with Spaniards, not Germans."

That cutting remark had the desired effect, and the men shifted uneasily in their chairs as they heard Garrote mutter "S'blood," as if someone had maligned his mother. At that, Diego Alatriste's pale green eyes showed the spark of a smile. That insult always worked a miracle; no further word of protest was heard among the veteran soldiers seated at the table, and the officer, now relaxed, was seen to return Alatriste's hint of a smile. Old dog to old dog.

"Your Mercies must leave immediately," Bragado said, ending the discussion.

Alatriste again stroked his mustache with two fingers. Then he turned to his comrades. "You heard the captain," he said.

The men began to get to their feet, Garrote grumbling,

the others resigned. Sebastián Copons—small, thin, knot-ted, and tough as an aged grapevine—had been on his feet for some time, buckling on his weapons without awaiting orders from anyone, as if all the delays, all the unpaid wages, even the very treasure of the king of Persia, all lead him to this miserable day: he, fatalist, like the Moors whose necks were being cut by his marauding ancestors a few centuries earlier. Diego Alatriste watched him put on his hat and cape and go outside to notify other soldiers of the squad who were quartered in the house next door. They had been together through many campaigns, from the days of Ostende to Fleurus and now Breda, and in all those years no one had heard more than thirty words from him.

"'Pon my soul, I almost forgot this," Bragado exclaimed.

He had picked up the jar of wine and was draining it, all the time eyeing the Flemish woman, who was cleaning scraps from the table. Without interrupting his drinking, holding the jug high, he dug into his doublet, pulled out a letter, and handed it to Diego Alatriste.

"This came for you a week ago."

The missive was closed with sealing wax and raindrops had slightly smeared the ink of the address. Alatriste read the name of the sender on the back: *From don Francisco de Quevedo Villegas, La Bardiza Inn, Madrid.*

As the woman passed by Alatriste without looking at him, one of her firm, full breasts brushed against him.

Steel glinted as it was slipped into scabbards, and well-oiled leather gleamed. Alatriste picked up his buffcoat and slowly belted it before asking for the baldric with his sword and dagger. Outside, rain continued to beat against the window panes.

"Two prisoners at least," Bragado insisted.

The men were ready: mustaches, beards, hats, folds of waxed capes covered with mended tears and clumsy patches; light arms, appropriate for the job they were about to do; no muskets or pikes or other impediments, only good and simple steel: swords and daggers from Toledo, Sahagún, Milan, and Biscay. Also an occasional pistol poked out of the wearer's clothing, but it would be useless with powder saturated by so much rain. Between them they also had a few crusts of bread and some rope to tie up Hollanders. And those empty, indifferent gazes of old soldiers prepared to face the hazards of their office once again before one day returning to their homeland marked by a crazy quilt of scars, with no bed to lie in or wine to drink and no hearth for baking their bread. And if they didn't achieve this, they would be what in soldier's cant were called *terratenientes*, landowners, claiming five feet of hard-fought Flemish soil in which they would find eternal sleep, with a hymn in praise of Spain forever on their lips.

Bragado finished his wine. Diego Alatriste accompanied him to the door, and the officer left without further conversation: no exchanges, no good-byes. The men watched their commander ride off down the dike on the back of his old field horse, crossing paths with Sebastián Copons, who was on his way back to the house.

Alatriste felt the woman's eyes on him, but he did not turn to look at her. Without explaining whether they were parting only for hours or forever, he pushed open the door and went out into the rain, immediately feeling water through the cracked soles of his boots. The wetness seeped into the marrow of his bones, stirring the aches of old wounds. He sighed quietly and began to walk, hearing his companions splashing through the mud behind him, following him in the direction of the dike where Copons was standing as motionless as a small, strong statue beneath the steady downpour.

"What a cesspool of a life," someone muttered.

And without further words, with heads lowered, wrapped in their soaked capes, the line of Spaniards faded into the gray landscape.

From don Francisco de Quevedo Villegas to don Alatriste y Tenorio* Tercio Viejo de Cartagena* Military post of Flanders

I hope, my esteemed captain, that upon receipt of the present you are, Y.M., healthy and of one piece.

In regard to my own condition, I am writing to you having recently emerged from an abominable flux of humors that, evincing itself in fevers, had laid me low for several days. Now, thanks to a merciful God, I am fine and can send you both my constant affection and my greetings.

I hazard that you are deeply engaged in the affair at Breda, which is a business that buzzes from mouth to mouth at Court because of its importance to the future of our monarchy and to the Catholic faith, and also because it is said that the military machine set in motion has seen no equal since the days when Julius Caesar besieged Alesia. Here it is ventured that the stronghold will be definitively won from the Dutch and that it will fall like a ripe plum . . . although there is always someone who points out that don Ambrosio Spínola is taking his time and that ripe fruit must be eaten in season or it becomes full of worms. Whatever the case, since you have never lacked a sturdy heart, I wish you good fortune in the assaults, trenches, mines, countermines, and other diabolical inventions that keep you engaged in such clamorous affairs.

Once, I heard Y.M. say that war is clean, and I understood your argument fully, to the point that

at times I cannot but consider you to be correct.
Here in La Villa y Corte, our city of Madrid,
the enemy does not wear breastplate and helmet
but, rather, toga, cassock, or silk doublet, and
he never attacks face on but prefers ambush. In
that particular, please know that everything is as it
has always been, only worse. I have faith still in
the intent of the conde-duque, but I fear that not
even his desires will prevail. We Spanish have
fewer tears than reasons to weep, for it is a vain
labor to offer light to the blind, words to the deaf,
science to the ignorant, and honor to monarchs.
Here the same types continue to flourish: the blond
and powerful caballero is still soldier, horse, and
king in any matter, and he who is honest does
naught but harm himself. As for me, I continue to
make no progress in my eternal suit concerning the
Torre de Juan Abad, each day battling this
wretched and venal legal system and its
practitioners that God, weary of confining
monstrosities to hell, instead visits upon us. And I
assure you, Capitán, that never before have I found
myself among such toads as those in the
Providencia square. And regarding that subject,
please allow me to regale you with a sonnet
inspired by my recent calamities:

You scatter judgments like grain tossed to geese,
selling the law you do not comprehend,
dispensing only what brings you gold, and
coveting, more than Jason, the Golden Fleece.

Both rights divine and those of mortal man
in your interpretation are debased,
and whether you are cruel, or affect grace,
each sentence is shrewdly tailored to your plan

Plaints of the poor you coldly set aside
Lending your ear only to he who pays:
personal gain, not rule of law, your guide.

And as your greed cannot be mollified,
either wash your hands, as Pilate did,
or hang like Judas, with coins but vilified.

I am still polishing the first line, but I have faith
that the sense will please you. As for other matters,
verses and earthly justice aside, all is going well.
At court, the star of your friend Quevedo is still
in the ascent, of which I make no complaint, and
I am again well regarded in the house of the
conde-duque and at the palace, perhaps because
in recent days I have guarded my tongue and put

*my sword into safekeeping, despite my natural
impulse to disencumber both one and the other.
But a man must live; and given that I know exile,
lawsuits, prisons, and affliction far too well,
I think it will not stain my reputation to allow
myself a truce and grant a period of quiet to my
elusive fortunes. For that reason, each day
I attempt to remember that one must proffer thanks
to kings and powerful men, though there be no
cause, and never voice a complaint, though there be
cause to spare.*

*But when I told you that I have kept my
Toledo blade safely put away, I did not tell you
the whole truth; in point of fact I unsheathed it
some days ago to strike, as one would a servant or
a lowlife, a certain servile and talentless poetaster,
one Garciposadas, who in a number of villainous
verses discredited poor Cervantes—may he reign
in glory—alleging that Cervantes wrote the*
Quijote *with his maimed hand, that it was an
insignificant work of little substance; poorly written
prose with little to claim it as literature, and that
many people read it speaks only of the tastes of
common people. He vowed that the book affords
little benefit and that tomorrow no one will
remember it. This knave, whose pen spews foul*

*venom, is a bosom friend of that sodomite Góngora,
which says it all.*

*One night, when I was more inclined to
philosophize with my wine than waste time on
swine, I met the varlet himself at the door of the
Longinos tavern, the famous gathering place for
Gongora's followers, the bulwark of resplendence,
tricliniums, purplessences, and umbrageous waves of
undulating sea. He was accompanied by two
sycophants who would grovel to carry his wine: the*
bachiller *Echevarría and the* licenciado *Ernesto
Ayala, schooled reprobates—the latter grander than
the first—who piss bile and maintain that the only
authentic poetry is the gibberish, that is the
Gongóberish, that no one but the select can
appreciate. That select few being, of course,
themselves and their companions. These coxcombs
spend their lives belittling what others write, though
they are incapable of stringing together fourteen
lines to make a sonnet themselves. I was there with
the Duque de Medinaceli and a number of young
masked caballeros, all of them from the
brotherhood of San Martín de Valdeiglesias, and we
spent a happy while trimming the ears of those
scoundrels (who, if truth be known, suffered no
more than a few scratches), until the catchpoles*

arrived to impose peace, and we departed, and that was the end of that.

Here's a truth, speaking as we were of lowlife. The news about the royal secretary, Luis de Alquézar, the man you so deeply admire, is that he continues to hold a privileged position in the palace, occupying himself with ever more important affairs of state, and that he, like everyone at court, is amassing a fortune at an outrageously rapid rate. As you know, he has a niece who by now is a very beautiful girl and is waiting upon the queen as one of her meninas. *In regard to the uncle, it is fortunate that you find yourself at some distance; upon your return from Flanders you must be on your guard against him. One never knows how far the poison spit by serpents will reach.*

And since I am speaking of serpents, I must tell Y.M. that some weeks ago I thought I saw that Italian with whom, I believe, you have unfinished business. I happened upon him in front of Lucio's hostelry on Cava Baja, and, if it were truly he, he seemed to be enjoying excellent health. Which causes me to reflect that he is recovering remarkably well from your most recent conversations. He looked at me for an instant as if he recognized me and then

went off down the street without a word. A sinister
individual, one might say in passing, dressed in
black from head to toe, with that pitted face and his
enormous sword hanging from his belt. Someone to
whom I discreetly mentioned the encounter told me
that he is the leader of a small band of thugs and
ruffians Alquézar keeps on a fixed wage, and who
act as his evangelists in sinister assaults. This is a
business, I venture, that Your Mercy will have to
face one day—one way or another—since he who
leaves the offender alive also leaves alive
his vengeance.

I continue to be a faithful patron of the Tavern
of the Turk, where your friends charge me with
wishing you well, and I send effusive greetings from
Caridad la Lebrijana, who, from what is said—and
I have no proof to say it is a lie—feels your absence
and reserves for you your old room on Calle del
Arcabuz. She is still in good health, one might
almost say in full bloom, which is not
inconsequential. Martín Saldaña is convalescing
from a nocturnal conflict with some ruffians who
were attempting to gain refuge in San Ginés. He
received a wound from one of their swords but will
certainly recover. It is said that he killed three.

I do not wish to rob you of more time. I ask only

that you transmit my affection to young Íñigo, who by now must be a fine young lad and gallant emulator of Mars, having as he has Y.M. to act as his spiritual guide, in the manner of Virgil and Achilles. Recall to him if you so please, my sonnet on youth and prudence, adding, again if it please you, these other verses with which I am still wrestling:

> *To the soldier, wounds are but misery,*
> *adding nothing to his true fame,*
> *nor does serving add glory to his name:*
> *naught but a chimera to warm his reverie....*

Although, what can I say about these things, esteemed captain, that Y.M. does not recognize to the fullest extent.

May God keep you in his care always, my friend.

Yours

Fran. de Quevedo Villegas

P.S. You are sorely missed on the steps of San Felipe and at performances of Lope's plays. I also forgot to tell you that I received a letter from a certain lad whom you may remember, the last of an

*unfortunate family. Apparently, after attending, in
his way, to unfinished matters in Madrid, he was
able to make his way to the Indies under an
assumed name. I imagined that you might be
pleased to hear that news.*

3. THE MUTINY

Later, after the bull had bolted from the pen, there was
great tattle and prattling about whether anyone had seen
it coming, but the pure truth is that no one did anything
to prevent it. The spark that set everything off was not the
Flanders winter, which was not especially severe that year.
There was no frost or snow, although the rains were a
major hardship aggravated by the lack of food, the diminished population in the villages, and our responsibilities
around Breda. But those things all come with the profession, and Spanish troops could endure the travails of war
with patience. Wages, however, were a different matter.
Many veterans had known poverty following their dis-
charge and the reforms brought about by the Twelve Years'
Truce with the Dutch; they knew in their bones that service in the name of our lord and king demanded a high

price when it came to dying but offered little reward when it came to surviving. And I have already noted on this subject that more than a few soldiers, whether they were old, mutilated, or with long campaign records stashed in the tubular containers they carried, had to beg in the streets and squares of our mean-spirited Spain, where again and again the same people amassed wealth while those who had given their health, blood, and life to preserve the true religion, the estates, and the wealth of our monarch remained buried and forgotten. There was hunger in Europe, in Spain, and in the military. The *tercios* had been waging war against the entire world for a long century and were beginning to not know precisely why, whether it was to defend indulgences or to enable the Court of Madrid to continue believing, amidst its balls and soirées, that it still ruled the world.

These men no longer had even the comfort of considering themselves professional because they weren't being paid, and there is nothing like hunger to undercut discipline and conscience. So the matter of arrears complicated the situation in Flanders; for if that winter some *tercios*, including those of allied nations, twice received half their wages, the Cartagena *tercio* never saw so much as an escudo. The reasons for that are not within my ken, although at the time it was attributed to bad administration of the finances of our colonel, don Pedro de la Daga, and to some obscure affair of lost or appropriated monies. The reality is that several of the fifteen Spanish, Italian, Burgundian, Walloon, and German *tercios* maintaining the tight circle around Breda under the direct supervision of don Ambrosio Spínola had some incentive, some hope, but ours, scattered in small advance postings outside the city, counted itself among the troops placed on a long financial fast by the king. It was creating a dangerous atmosphere; for as Lope wrote in *El asalto de Mastrique* (The Attack on Mastrique):

> *As long as a man is not yet dead*
> *always give him drink and bread;*
> *is there naught but plodding on*
> *endlessly, with all hope gone?*
> *I have honored that tattered banner,*
> *But no man should suffer in this manner,*
> *So, for God or king, hear what I say,*
> *I'll not go hungry another day!*

Add to that the fact that our deployment along the banks of the Ooster canal was in the closest position to the enemy, and therefore the most vulnerable to attack. We knew that Maurice of Nassau, general of the rebellious estates, was raising an army to come to the aid of Breda, within which another Nassau, Justin, was holding out with forty-seven companies of Hollanders, French, and English. These latter nations were, as Your Mercies are aware, always right in the thick of things when the opportunity arose to dip their bread in our stewpot. Indisputable was the fact that the army of the Catholic king was walking on the edge of a very sharp sword, twelve hours' march from the nearest loyal cities, while the Dutch were but three or four hours from theirs. The Cartagena *tercios'* orders were to thwart every attack that sought to approach our troops from the rear, thus assuring that our comrades entrenched around Breda would have time to prepare for any onslaught and not be forced to withdraw in shame or be drawn into an unequal battle. That placed a few squads in the scattered alignment that, in military jargon, was called the *centinela perdida* (the assignment of "forlorn hope"), advance units whose mission was to sound the call to arms but whose chances of surviving were summed up nicely by the pessimistic phrase "in the line of duty." Captain Bragado's *bandera* had been chosen for that task, as they were long-suffering, experienced in the misery of war, and capable—with or without leaders or officers—of fighting on a small stretch of land when the odds were stacked against them. But perhaps too much was riding on the patience of a few, and I must, in all justice, say that Colonel don Pedro de la Daga, maliciously called Jiñalasoga, was the one who precipitated the conflict with his imperious behavior . . . highly improper in a man well born and commander of a Spanish *tercio.*

I well remember that on that fateful day there was some sun, though it was Dutch sun and that I was busy making the most of it. I was sitting on a stone bench near the gate of the house and read, with great pleasure and benefit, a book Captain Alatriste used to lend me so that I could practice. It was a worn first edition, with countless signs of mold and rough treatment, of the first part of *El ingenioso hidalgo don Quijote de la Mancha.* It had been printed in Madrid during the fifth year of the century—only six years before I was born—by Juan de la Cuesta. It was a wondrous book by the good don Miguel de Cervantes, who was an inspired genius and ill-starred compatriot. Had he been born English, or one of those accursed Frenchies, the cock would have crowed a different tune for this illustrious, one-armed man during his lifetime, and not just to give him posthumous glory, a fate that a begrudging nation like ours tends to reserve for good and decent people, especially in the best of cases. I was fascinated by the book, its adventures and happenings, and moved by the sublime madness of the last *caballero andante*, the gallant Don Quijote, and also by the knowledge—Diego Alatriste had apprised me of this—that during the most exalted moments the centuries had ever seen, when galleys laden with Spanish infantrymen confronted the fearsome Turkish armada in the Gulf of Lepanto, one of the valiant men who fought with sword in hand that day had been don Miguel, a poor and loyal soldier of his country, of his God, and of his king, as Diego Alatriste and my father later became, and as I myself proposed to be.

I was that morning, as I was saying, reading in the sunshine and pausing from time to time to consider some of the meaty arguments proposed. I, too, had my Dulcinea, as perhaps some of Your Mercies may recall, although my travails of love came not from the disdain of the mistress of my heart but from her perfidy, a circumstance of which I have previously given account when narrating earlier adventures. But even though I had seen myself on the verge of sacrificing honor and life in that sweet trap—the memory of a certain vile talisman sears my memory—I could not forget the vision of blonde corkscrew curls and eyes as blue as the sky over Madrid or of a smile identical to the devil's when, through Eve's intercession, he tempted Adam to sink his teeth into the fabled apple. The object of my concerns, I calculated, must by now be about thirteen or fourteen years old, and when I imagined her at court participating in soirées and flirtatious carriage rides, surrounded by pages and handsome youths and dandies, I felt for the first time the black scourge of jealousy. Not even my youth, ever more vigorous, or the portents and perils of Flanders, or the nearby presence of the army of vivandières and trulls who followed the soldiers, or the Flemish women themselves—to whom, by my faith, we Spaniards were not always as hostile as we were to their fathers, brothers, and husbands—could make me forget Angélica de Alquézar.

I was mulling over these thoughts when a variety of sounds and commotion drew me from my reading. A general muster of the *tercio* had been issued, and soldiers were running hither and yon collecting weapons and appurtenances. The colonel had summoned the troops to a flat area just outside Oudkerk, which town we had taken by force some time back and turned into the principal quarters of the Spanish garrison northwest of Breda. My comrade, Jaime Correas, who showed up with the men from Lieutenant Coto's squad, told me as we joined the others on the way to the appointed location, about a mile from Oudkerk, that the review of the troops had been ordered overnight, called to resolve some very ugly questions of discipline involving a confrontation between soldiers and officers the previous day. This was the rumor circulating among the troops and the *mochileros* as we walked along the dike toward the nearby plain. The subject was being discussed from every viewpoint, and commands occasionally shouted by the sergeants were not enough to quiet the men.

Jaime, walking beside me, was carrying two short pikes, a brass helmet weighing twenty pounds, and a musket from the squad he served. I myself had Diego Alatriste's and Mendieta's harquebuses, a calfskin pack stuffed to the top, and several flasks of powder. Jaime was bringing me up to date as we walked along. It seems that in light of the need to fortify Oudkerk with bastions and trenches, regular soldiers had been asked to do the job, digging sod and carrying fascines (bundles of sticks to aid fortification) for the battlements, with the promise of pay that would remedy the poverty in which, as I have said, they all found themselves because of wages owed and scarcity of provisions. Put a different way, wages to which they were entitled but had not received could be earned a second time by those willing to put shoulder to the wheel, and at the end of each day's labor they would receive the agreed-upon stipend. Many in the *tercio* accepted this means of improving their situation, but some spoke up, saying that if there was good coin to be had, their back pay should come first and then the fortifications and that they should not have to work to earn what was already owed them by rights. They said they would rather go without than resort to this remedy, forcing hunger to compete so vilely with honor and that a hidalgo—for every soldier called himself that—deserved more and that it was better to die of misery and maintain their good name than to owe their well-being to spades and hoes.

In the midst of all this commotion, groups of men had been milling around and trading words amongst themselves, when a sergeant from a certain company mistreated a harquebusier from the *bandera* of Captain Torralba. This soldier and a comrade, short-tempered despite recognizing by his halberd that the aggressor was a sergeant, jumped into the fire, and, wielding their swords a little too freely, they gravely wounded their offender, only a miracle preventing them from dispatching him to his reward. So it was expected that the colonel would make a public example of the guilty parties and that, with the exception of those on watch, he wanted the entire *tercio* to witness it.

In these and related discussions we *mochileros* made our way along with the troops, and even in the squad of Diego Alatriste I heard different views about the affair: Curro Garrote being the most stirred up and, as usual, Sebastián Copons the most indifferent. From time to time I shot uneasy looks at my master to see if I could read his opinion, but he was walking along without a word, as if he heard nothing: sword and dagger in his belt, and the tail of his short cape swinging to the rhythm of his steps. He was tight-lipped when anyone spoke to him, and his face was unreadable beneath the wide brim of his hat.

"Hang them!" said don Pedro de la Daga.

In the eerie silence of the esplanade, the colonel's voice sounded sharp and cold. The companies were aligned to form three sides of a great rectangle with the banner of each in the center: pike men and *coseletes* (soldiers so-called because of the armor they wore) lining the sides and detachments of harquebusiers at each corner. The twelve hundred soldiers of the *tercio* were so quiet and motionless that a botfly could have been heard among the rows. Under different circumstances it would have been a beautiful sight: all those men lined up with such precision, not sumptuously dressed, it is true—their clothing was covered with patches that at times were no more than rags, and they were even more poorly shod—but their weapons were oiled in accord with regulations, and their breastplates, helmets, pike heads, and harquebus barrels had been conscientiously cleaned and polished. *Mucrone corusco,* "with shining sword," the chaplain of the *tercio*, Padre Salanueva, would undoubtedly have said, had he been sober. Every man was wearing or, rather, had sewed onto his doublet or buffcoat, as I had, the faded *aspa*, (the crimson cross of Saint Andrew also known as the cross of Burgundy) an insignum that allowed Spaniards to recognize a fellow soldier in combat. And on the fourth side of the rectangle, next to the flag of the *tercio* itself, surrounded by his principal officers and the six German halberdiers of his personal guard, was don Pedro de la Daga on horseback, his proud head bare, lace collar white against his tooled cuirass, cuisses of good Milanese steel, damascened sword at his side, antelope gloves, right hand on his hip and reins in his left.

"From a dead tree," he added.

Then, with a flick of the reins, he made his mount wheel and spin to face each of the twelve companies of the *tercio*, as if defying any inclination to discuss his order, which added to a dishonorable death by hanging the insult that the adjudged would not swing from a leafy green branch. I was with the other *mochileros*, close behind the troop formation, keeping our distance from the women, the curious, and the rabble watching the spectacle from afar. I was a few paces behind Diego Alatriste's squad, and I could see some of the soldiers in the last rows, Garrote among them, mumbling under their breath when they heard de la Daga's words. As for Alatriste, his eyes were fixed on the colonel, and his face was as emotionless as ever.

Don Pedro de la Daga must have been about fifty, a small man from Valladolid, with bright eyes, a quick wit, and long experience in the military, though little esteemed by his troops. It was said that his sour temperament came from bilious humors, that is, a constipated nature. A favorite of our General Spínola and with influential patrons in Madrid, de la Daga had made his reputation as a sergeant-major in the Palatinate campaign and had been granted command of the Cartagena *tercio* after a falconet ball blew off don Enrique Monzón's leg in Fleurus. Jiñalasoga was not a nickname someone dreamed up out of nowhere; our *maestre* was one of those men who, like Tiberius, chose to be despised and feared by his men, using such means to impose discipline. That he was courageous in battle was indisputable. He scorned danger as he did his soldiers (you recall that his personal escort consisted of German halberdiers), and he had a good head for strategy. He was close-fisted with money, sparing with favors, and cruel with punishment.

When the two prisoners heard the sentence, they showed little reaction; they already knew the outcome of the affair; not even they could get away with running through a sergeant. The rules of the game were clearly established. The two men stood in the center of the rectangle, guarded by the chief bailiff of the *tercio*, both bareheaded and their hands tied behind their backs. One was older and had many scars, gray hair, and an enormous mustache; he was the one who had made the first move against their victim, and seemed the calmer of the two. The second was somewhat younger, thin, heavily bearded, and while the elder man kept looking up to the sky, as if none of this had anything to do with him, the thinner one showed more signs of dejection, looking down at the ground, then toward his comrades, then at the hooves of the colonel's horse only a short distance away. But, like his companion, he comported himself well.

At a signal from the bailiff there was a drum roll, and don Pedro de la Daga's bugler blasted a few notes to seal the matter.

"Do the adjudged have anything to say?"

A shiver of expectation ran through the companies, and the forest of pikes seemed to tilt forward, the way the wind bows grain, as those holding them leaned in, trying to hear. Then we all watched the bailiff, who had approached the prisoners, tilt his head to one side and listen to something the elder of the two was saying. He looked toward the colonel, who nodded assent, not out of benevolence but because it was the traditional protocol. Then those of us on the esplanade heard the gray-haired man say that he was an old soldier and, like his comrade, a man who had performed his duty up to the present day. Dying went with the profession, but to die of rope fever— whether from a green or dead or devil-may-take-it limb didn't matter, *pardiez*—was an unfitting insult to soldiers like themselves who had always put their legs into their breeches like true men. So, seeing that they were to be shuffled off this coil, he and his comrade were asking if it could be by harquebus ball, the way a Spaniard and man of courage dies, not hanged like peasants. And if in the end it was the cost that was the essential factor, he would provide the balls for the harquebuses and save the good colonel the expense. His own were cast from good Escombreras lead, surplus from provisions that he kept in his powder flask, and they wouldn't do him any damn good where he was going. But be it known, he said, no matter the method, rope or harquebus or singing camp songs, his comrades and he were being sent on their way with a half year of lost pay still owed to them.

Once he had spoken, the veteran shrugged his shoulders with a resigned air and stoically spat on the ground between his boots. His companion spat too, and there were no further words. A long silence ensued, and then, from high atop his horse, don Pedro de la Daga, still with his fist on his hip and not moved in the least by the request, repeated, unrelenting, "Hang them!" At that, a clamor arose from among the various *banderas* that set the officers on their heels, and there was agitation in the rows of soldiers. Some even fell out of line and shouted, and no orders from the sergeants and captains could put an end to the tumult. Watching all this uproar open-mouthed, I turned toward Captain Alatriste to see which side he was taking. He was shaking his head very slowly, as if he had lived through all of this before.

The mutinies in Flanders, offspring of poor discipline de-
riving from bad administration, were the illness that
sapped the prestige of the Spanish monarchy, whose decline
in the rebellious provinces—even in those that remained
loyal—owed more to mutinous troops than to the actual
conduct of the war. Already in my time, insurrection was
the one sure way to collect wages. The mutineers would
take a city and barricade themselves inside it; indeed some
of the worst sacking in all of Flanders came at the hands
of troops seeking compensation for unpaid wages. In any
case, it is fair to point out that we were not the only ones.
For if we Spanish, as patient as we were cruel, resorted to
blood and fire, the Walloon, Italian, and German troops did
the same, and they reached the peak of infamy when they
sold the forts of San Andrés and Crevecoeur to the enemy,
something the Spanish never did. It was not that they were
not willing, but they preferred to avoid shame and
preserve their reputations. S'blood! It is one thing to kill
and sack over not being paid, but treachery and acts
affecting honor are a different matter.

And on the subject of honor, there were still examples
as memorable as the business at Cambrai, where things
had come to such a disastrous point that the Conde de
Fuentes had to ask the soliders, the "caballeros" of troops

then mutinying at Tirlemont, in his most solicitous tones "to be so kind as to assist him" in taking the stronghold. That horde suddenly became a disciplined and fearsome force again and attacked in perfect order, capturing the citadel and the plaza. And it was mutinous troops who bore the worst of the fight in the dunes of Nieuport, where they requested the position of greatest danger because a woman, the *infanta* Clara-Eugenia, had asked for their help. And I should not overlook the mutinies in Alost, where men had refused to accept the conditions offered in person by the Conde de Mansfeld and had allowed to pass, unhindered, several Dutch regiments that were about to wreak terrible damage to the king's estates. Those same troops, when finally they received pay and saw that it was not payment in full, would not accept a single *maravedí*, refusing to fight even though Flanders, Europe itself, was being lost. However, when they learned that in Antwerp six thousand Dutch and fourteen thousand civilians were about to exterminate the one hundred and thirty Spaniards defending the castle, they set out at forced march at three in the morning, crossed the Escalda, placed green twigs in their helmets as an indication that they anticipated victory, and swore either to eat with Christ in Paradise that night or take their supper in Antwerp. In the end, as their lieu-tenant, Juan de Navarrete, knelt on the counterscarp wav-ing their banner back and forth, they yelled, "Santiago and Spain!" arose as one, and, rushing the Dutch trenches, they stabbed, slit throats, and crushed the heads of any being in their path. In short, they did what they had sworn to do. Juan de Navarrete and another fourteen did in fact dine with Christ—or with whomever courageous men who die on their feet dine with—but the remainder of their comrades ate that night in Antwerp. For if it is all too true that though our poor Spain has never known justice, or good government, or honest public servants, and has been granted kings barely worthy of wearing the crown, she has also never, as God is my witness, lacked for subjects willing to overlook indifference, poverty, and injustice, willing to and clench their teeth, unsheathe steel, and fight for the honor of their nation. For when all is said and done, Spain's honor was the sum of the negligible honor of each individual.

But let us return to Oudkerk. That was the first of the many mutinies that I would witness during the twenty years of adventure and military life that would take me to the last stand of the Spanish infantry at Rocroi, the day when Spain's sun finally set in Flanders. During the time of my story, this kind of disorder had become a common institution among our troops, and the process, dating back even further than the days of the great emperor Charles V, was carried out in accord with a well-known and precise ritual. So that day men in some of the few companies began yelling "Pay, Pay," and others joined in with "Mutiny, Mutiny." And the first company, that of Captain Torralba, the one to which the two condemned men belonged, contributed their part to the furor. Prior to this moment there had been no handbills or conspiracy, so events developed spontaneously. Opinions were divided: Some were on the side of maintaining discipline, while others touted open rebellion. But what truly aggravated matters was the character of our colonel. Another more flexible man would have set one candle to God and one to the devil, placating both sides, and soothed the soldiers with words they wanted to hear, for never, that I am aware, did words wound a miser where it hurts most: in his purse. I am referring to something in the vein of "My sons," "My gallant soldiers," words of that nature, which had been skillfully employed by the Duque de Alba, don Luis de Requesens, and Alejandro Farnesio, who at heart were as inflexible and scornful of their troops as don Pedro de la Daga was of his. But Jiñalasoga was faithful to his sobriquet, and he made it abundantly clear that he did not give a fig about anything his "gallant soldiers" might do or say. So he ordered the bailiff and his German escort to lead the two prisoners to the nearest tree, dead or green, it was all the same to him. Then he ordered his personal company, one hundred-plus harquebusiers whom he, the colonel, commanded directly, to go to the center of the rectangle with cords lighted and balls in the barrel. This unit, which had also not been paid but which did enjoy certain privileges, obeyed without argument. That fired up spirits even more.

In truth, only about a fourth of the soldiers wanted to mutiny, but the agitators were scattered throughout the *banderas*, calling for insurrection, and many men could not make up their minds. In ours, Curro Garrote was the one fueling the disorder, finding a chorus in no few comrades, which, despite the efforts of Captain Bragado, threatened to break up the entire formation, as was already happening in some of the other companies. We *mochileros* ran to our own, determined not to be left out, and Jaime Correas and I pushed through the soldiers who were shouting in all the tongues of Spain, some with steel already bared in their hands. As usual, according to their tongues and lands of origin, men were lining up against one another: Valencians on one side and Andalucians on the other; Leonese confronting Castilians and Galicians; Cataláns, Basques, and Aragonese looking out for themselves and their interests; and the Portuguese, of whom there were a few, watching the groups form and having no part of it.

As a result, there were no two kingdoms or regions in agreement. Looking back, there is no way to explain the

Reconquest other than by the fact that the Moors themselves were Spanish. As for Captain Bragado, he had a pistol in one hand and a dagger in the other, and with Lieutenant Coto and Second Lieutenant Minaya, who was the company standard bearer, he was trying to restore calm but with no success at all. From company to company you could begin to hear cries of "*Guzmanes* out!" This stage of banishing the nobles who were their commanders was a significant aspect of a curious phenomenon that arose during such insurrections. Soldiers always made a gala display of the status they derived from their profession, calling themselves *hijosdalgos*, men of quality, and they always wanted to make it clear that the mutiny was against their leaders, not the authority of the Catholic king. So, in order to avoid indicting that authority and dishonoring the *tercio*, a mutual accord was reached between troops and officers that allowed the latter to march out with their flags along with individual soldiers who chose not to disobey. In that way, officers and insignia were left without stain on their honor, the *tercio* with its reputation intact, and those mutinying could later make a disciplined return to serve the authority that they had never formally renounced. No one wanted a repeat of what had happened to the Leiva *tercio*, which was dissolved in Tilte following a mutiny, when tearful standard bearers burned their staffs and banners rather than surrender them, veteran soldiers bared chests riddled with scars, captains threw their broken cavalry lances to the ground, and all those rough and formidable men wept from shame and dishonor.

Bowing to tradition, Captain Bragado, with great reluctance, broke from formation, taking with him the unit's banner, Soto, Minaya, the sergeants, and the few corporals and soldiers who followed. Jaime Correas, enchanted with the pandemonium, ran from one side to the other, finally joining in the call for "Guzmanes out!" I too was fascinated with all the uproar, and at one moment yelled along with everyone else, although I stopped when I saw that the officers were actually leaving the company. As for Diego Alatriste, I can report that I had found a place near him and his friends in the squad. His face was grave; he had placed his harquebus butt down on the ground and was standing with both hands resting on the mouth of the barrel. In his group, no one was talking, nor did they seem in any way perturbed, the exception being Garrote, who had already fallen in with the other soldiers and was singing the lead part. When finally Bragado and the officers left, my master turned to Mendieta, Rivas, and Llop, who shrugged their shoulders and, without any fuss, joined the group of mutineers. Copons, however, started after the flag and the officers without a comment to anyone. Alatriste breathed a quiet sigh, shouldered his harquebus, and followed Copons. It was then that he noticed that I was right beside him, thrilled to be in the middle of things and with no intention whatsoever of leaving. He gave me a pinch on the nape of my neck that I won't forget, forcing me to follow him.

"Your king is your king," he said.

He threaded his way among soldiers who stepped aside to let him pass, and as they watched him leave, no one dared offer a reproach. Once the two of us were out on open ground, we found ourselves near a group of ten or twelve men composed of Bragado and his loyal soldiers, although, like Copons, who stood there without a word as if this had nothing to do with him, Alatriste kept himself a little apart, almost halfway between the loyalists and the company. Alatriste again set his harquebus on the ground, placed his hands over the mouth of the barrel, and with the shadow of his hat rim shading his gray-green eyes, stood stock still, taking everything in.

Jiñalasoga was still as unyielding as iron. The German guards were stringing up the two prisoners amid the riotous clamor of the troops, whose officers, with their banners, had already separated from their units. I could count four companies that were mutinying among the twelve that formed the *tercio*, and the rebels were beginning to group together with yells and threats. I heard a shot, though I have no idea who fired it, and it hit no one. Then the colonel ordered his *bandera* to aim harquebuses and muskets in the direction of the mutineers and the loyal soldiers to reposition themselves in his ranks. There were orders, drum rolls, and bugles, and don Pedro de la Daga spurred his horse, sprinting from one side of the field to the other, readying his troops for battle. I have to acknowledge that he showed a lot of backbone, for malcontents could easily have sprayed a shower of harquebus shots that would have left him at the end of *his* rope. Being courageous and being a whoreson are not always mutually exclusive. Loyal companies were maneuvered into positions facing the rebel soldiers, albeit with manifest reluctance. Then there were more drums and bugles, orders to officers and loyal soldiers to join companies already in formation, and Bragado and the others fell into line. Copons was beside Diego Alatriste and me, but as I said, somewhat apart from the others. And on hearing the order and affirming that the *tercio* was in place facing the rebels, weapons in hand and slow matches smoking, the two veterans laid their harquebuses on the ground, took off the bandoliers containing twelve charges of powder—the belts they called "the twelve apostles"— and thus stripped of weapons, set off behind their banner.

I had never seen anything like it. As the soldiers loyal to the *tercio* took up battle positions, the four mutinying companies took theirs. They, too, adopted battle formation: pike men in the center and detachments of harquebuses in the corners. In the absence of officers, squad corporals, even ordinary soldiers, took command. With the natural instinct of veterans, the mutineers were aware that lack of order would be their ruin, and that—now here's a military paradox—only discipline could save. So that without standing down a point, they executed their maneuvers according to traditional patterns, one by one slipping into place in line. Soon we smelled the unmistakable odor of lit saltpeter-soaked harquebus cords and saw forks for the muskets set into the ground, preparing the weapons to be fired.

The colonel was determined to have either blood or obedience. The two sentenced men were already hanging from a tree, and with that matter resolved, the German escorts—tall, blond, and as unfeeling as slabs of meat—again surrounded don Pedro de la Daga, halberds upraised. Their leader gave new orders, the drums, bugles, and fifes sounded one more time, and still with that irritating right fist planted on his hip, Jiñalasoga watched as his loyal companies began to advance toward the mutineers.

"Cartagena *tercio*! Haaaalt!"

Suddenly everything went silent. Loyal and rebel companies were in close rows some twenty-five meters apart, pikes at the ready and harquebuses loaded. The banners removed from mutinying units joined together the center of the formation, along with the loyal soldiers escorting them.

I was right among them, for I wanted to stand beside my master, who had taken his place with the dozen men in his company who had not chosen the other side. With no harquebus, his sword in its scabbard, and his thumbs hooked into his belt, Diego Alatriste gave the impression he was merely an observer; nothing in his attitude indicated that he was prepared to attack his former companions.

"Cartagena *tercio*! Reaaaaaady harquebuses!"

Down the rows echoed the metallic sounds of harquebusiers packing powder into the pans and smoldering cord in the striker. Through the grayish smoke from the ignited cords I could see the faces of the men we were confronting: tanned, bearded, scarred, with expressions of grim resolve beneath their helmets and ripped hat brims. Triggered by the movements of our harquebusiers, some on the rebel side made the same preparations, and many of the *coseletes* in the first rows set their pikes. But cries and protests could be heard among them—"*Señores, señores*, let us use reason!"—and nearly all the harquebuses and pikes of the mutineers were again held upright, giving to understand that it was not their intention to attack their companions. On our side, we all turned to look at de la Daga when his voice resounded across the open field.

"Sergeant-major! Make those men swear obedience to their king."

Sergeant-Major Idiáquez stepped forward, baton in

hand, and demanded that the rebels immediately renounce their demands. It was a mere formality, and Idiáquez, a veteran who had mutinied no few times himself—especially in the year 1598, when unpaid wages and lack of discipline had caused us to lose half of Flanders—intervened briefly and succinctly, returning to our lines without waiting for a reply. For their part, none of the men in front of us seemed to grant any importance to the command the sergeant major had issued, and all we heard were isolated cries of "Pay! Pay!" After which, as erect as ever in his saddle and implacable in his tooled cuirass, don Pedro de la Daga lifted one antelope-gloved hand.

"Aimmm harquebuses!

The harquebusiers set their weapons against their cheeks, finger on the trigger of the striker, and blew on the lit cords. The heavier fork-mounted muskets were pointed straight at the opposing ranks, where some were beginning to stir in their lines, restless but with no signs of hostility.

"Order to fire! At my command!"

That command boomed across the esplanade, and although some few men in the rebel lines stepped back, I must say that nearly all were dauntless, remaining in place despite the menacing barrels of the loyalists' harquebuses. I glanced at Diego Alatriste and saw that like most of the soldiers, both those holding weapons on our side and those

facing us, stoically waiting to be fired upon, he was looking toward Sergeant-Major Idiáquez. The captains and sergeants of the companies were also looking toward him,
but he in turn had his eye on his most supreme excellency
the colonel. Who was not looking at anyone, as if he were
engaged in an exercise he simply found annoying. Jiñalasoga had already lifted his hand when we all saw—or
thought we saw—Idiáquez give a slight negative shake of
his head, barely a movement that could not really be called
a movement, and therefore it could not be said to contradict discipline, so later, when responsible parties made their
inquiries, no one could swear he had seen it. And with that
gesture, just at the instant don Pedro de la Daga called
"Fire!" the eight loyal companies lowered their pikes and
the harquebusiers as a single man and laid their weapons
on the ground.

4. TWO VETERANS

It took three days of negotiation, half payment of back wages, and a personal appearance from our General don Ambrosio Spínola to restore obedience among the Oudkerk mutineers. Three days in which the discipline of the old Cartagena *tercio* was more iron-fisted than ever, with officers and standards of all the companies gathered together in the town and the *tercio* itself camped outside the walls. I have already reported how the *tercios* were never more disciplined than when they were mutinying. On this occasion they even reinforced the advanced watch posts to prevent the Dutch from taking advantage of circumstances and falling upon us like pigs on grain. As for the soldiers, the system of order established by elected representatives functioned very efficiently and without oversight, even going so far as to execute, this time without protest from anyone, five scruffy miscreants who had thought they could sack the town on their own. They were reported by citizens, and in a summary trial, before a tribunal composed of their fellow soldiers, they were sentenced to be shot in front of the cemetery wall, where they would find peace and later glory. In fact, at first there were only four men, but two other criminals guilty of lesser crimes had been sentenced to have their ears cut off, and one of them protested the judgment with many "'Pon my lifes" and "'Fore Gods," averring that a hidalgo and old Christian like himself, a descendent of Mendozas and Guzmans, would rather see himself dead than suffer such insult. So, the tribunal—unlike our commander and being composed of soldiers and comrades—was understanding on points of honor and decided to show mercy upon the ear, exchanging it for the ball from a harquebus and without according the scoundrel the change of heart—he was no doubt a fickle hidalgo—that overcame him when he found himself with both ears intact by the cemetery wall.

That was the first time I saw don Ambrosio Spínola y Grimaldi, otherwise known as Marqués de las Balbases, grandée of Spain, captain of the Flanders forces, whose image—wearing blued gold-studded armor, a general's baton in his left hand, large white collar of Flemish lace, red sash, and antelope boots, courteously preventing the conquered Dutchman from bowing before him—would live forever in history thanks to the brushes of Diego Velázquez. I will speak more of that famous painting when the time comes, for it is not irrelevant that it was I who, years later, provided the painter with the details he required.

At the time of Oudkerk and Breda our general was fifty-five or fifty-six years old, slim in body and face, pale, with gray beard and hair. His astute and resolute character was not at odds with his Genoese homeland, which he had left by choice in order to serve our kings. A patient soldier favored by fate, he did not have the charisma of the iron man the Duque de Alba, nor the cunning of some of his other ancestors. His enemies at court, a number that increased with each of his successes—it could be no other way among Spaniards—had accused him both of being a foreigner and of becoming overly ambitious. But the indisputable fact was that he had achieved Spain's grandest military triumphs in the Palatinate and in Flanders, investing his personal fortune in those successes and mortgaging his family estates to pay his troops. He even lost his brother Federico in a naval battle against rebellious Hollanders. In that period his military prestige was enormous, to the degree that when Mauricio de Nassau, a general in the enemy camp, was asked who was the best soldier of the era, he had replied, "Spínola is the second." Our don Ambrosio was a man with a great deal of backbone, which had earned him a reputation among the troops in campaigns prior to the Twelve Years' Truce. Diego Alatriste could give personal testimony to that from his own memories of Spínola when he came to lend aid at Sluys, and also during the siege of Ostende. In the latter, the marqués had been in such a dangerous position in the midst of the fray that the soldiers, Alatriste among them, lowered their pikes and harquebuses, refusing to fight until their general took himself to a place of safety.

The day that don Ambrosio Spínola personally broke up the mutiny, many of us watched him as he emerged from the campaign tent where the negotiations had been carried out. His staff and our colonel, hanging his head, filed out behind him. De la Daga was chewing the ends of his mustache, furious that his proposal of hanging one of every ten mutineers to serve as a lesson had not been accepted. But don Ambrosio, with his intelligence and good nature, had declared the matter closed, restoring the formal discipline of the *tercios* and returning officers and banners to their companies. Eager soldiers lined up before the tables of the paymasters—the money had come from the private coffers of the general—and from all around the camp, sutlers, prostitutes, merchants, and other parasites of war flocked to receive their share of the torrent of gold.

Diego Alatriste was among those in the vicinity of the

tent. For this reason, when don Ambrosio Spínola came out, pausing a moment to allow his eyes to adjust to the light, the notes of the bugle drew Alatriste and his companions in closer in order to get a good look at the general. As was the custom among the old soldiers, most of them had brushed their oft-mended clothing; their weapons were polished; and even their hats seemed dashing despite stitched tears and holes, for these soldiers who took pride in their way of life were eager to demonstrate that a mutiny was not without its touches of gallantry among the men. This produced a strange paradox: Seldom had the soldiers of the Cartagena *tercio* looked better than when viewed by their general at the conclusion of the events at Oudkerk. And Spínola—Golden Fleece gleaming upon his gorget, escorted by his select harquebusiers and trailed by his staff, seemed to appreciate the sight as he strolled among the clusters of men who fell back to open a path for him and cheered him wildly just for being who he was and especially for delivering their pay. They also cheered to emphasize the contrast between him and don Pedro de la Daga, who was walking behind his captain-general and stewing over not having an excuse to illustrate the charms of his rope. There was, too, the sting of the admonishment that don Ambrosio had administered to him in private and in great detail, threatening to remove him from his command if he did not care for his soldiers as he would "little girls who were the light of his eyes." This is precisely what we heard from those who knew, although I doubt the part about the little girls. Everyone knows that compassionate or tyrannical, stupid or wise, all generals and colonels are dogs from the same litter and that none has the least concern for the soldiers, whose unique purpose in their minds is to garner them gold medallions and laurel wreaths. But that day the Spaniards, happy about the felicitous outcome of their mutiny, were ready to accept any rumor and any development. Don Ambrosio was smiling paternally left and right, greeting "his gallant soldiers" and "his sons," saluting genially from time to time with his baton and occasionally, when he recognized the face of an officer or veteran soldier, devoting a few courteous words directly to him. In short, he was doing his job. And by my faith, he was doing it well.

Then he came to Captain Alatriste, who was standing apart with his comrades watching the general's progress. It is true that the group was a striking sight, for as I have written, my master's squad was composed almost entirely of veteran soldiers, men with copious mustaches and scars on skin like Cordovan leather. Especially attired in all their trappings—bandoliers with the "twelve apostles," sword, dagger, harquebus or musket in hand—no one would question that there was no Dutchman or Turk or creature from hell who could stop them once the drums beat the tattoo to charge and give no quarter. Don Ambrosio looked the squad over, admiring the picture they made, and was about to smile and walk on by when he recognized my master, stopped, and said in his soft Spanish with its Italian cadences, "*Pardiez*, Captain Alatriste. Is it really you? I thought we had left you behind forever in Fleurus."

Alatriste doffed his hat and stood with it in his left hand, the wrist of his right draped over the barrel of his harquebus.

"Nearly so," Alatriste replied in measured tones, "as Your Excellency does me the honor of recalling. But it was not my hour."

The general studied the scars on the veteran's weathered face. He had first spoken to Alatriste twenty years before, during his attempt to save the day at Sluys when, surprised by a cavalry charge, don Ambrosio had had to take refuge in the square formed by Alatriste and other soldiers. Alongside them, his rank forgotten, the illustrious Genoese had had to fight for his life on foot, using only sword and pistol, throughout an endless day. He had not forgotten that, and nor had Alatriste.

"So I see," said Spínola. "And in those hedgerows of Fleurus, don Gonzalo de Córdoba told me that you fought like men of honor."

"Don Gonzalo spoke the truth when he used the word

honor, for honors were due. Nearly all my comrades stayed there."

Spínola scratched his goatee, as if he had just remembered something.

"Did I not promote you to sergeant at that time?"

Alatriste slowly shook his head. "No, Excellency. The 'sergeant' came about in '18, because Your Excellency remembered me from Sluys."

"Then how is it that you are a foot soldier once again?"

"I lost my rank a year later, because of a duel."

"Something serious?"

"A lieutenant."

"Dead?"

"As a doornail."

The general considered Alatriste's words and then exchanged a look with the officers surrounding him. He frowned and made a move to walk on.

"As God is my witness," he said, "I am surprised they didn't hang you."

"It was during the Maastrique mutiny, Excellency."

Alatriste had spoken without a shred of emotion. The general stopped, thinking back.

"Ah, yes, I remember now." The frown had disappeared, and he was smiling again. "The Germans and the colonel whose life you saved. And for that did I not grant you a warrant of eight *escudos?*"

Again Alatriste shook his head.

"No, Excellency. That was for White Mountain. When, with Captain Bragado, who is standing over there today, we climbed behind Bucquoi up to the forts above. As for the *escudos*, they were cut back to four."

At that, don Ambrosio's smile slipped from his face. He looked around with a distracted air.

"Well," he concluded. "At any rate, I am pleased to have seen you again. Is there anything I can do for you?"

Alatriste smiled, though his face changed very little; a barely perceptible light glinted among the wrinkles about his eyes.

"I think not, Excellency. Today I am collecting six months of back pay, and I have no complaint."

"Good. And this meeting between two old veterans has been pleasant, don't you agree?" He had put out a hand as if to give Alatriste a friendly pat on the shoulder, but the captain's steady and sardonic gaze appeared to dissuade him. "I am referring to you and me, of course."

"Naturally, Excellency."

"Soldier and, ahem, soldier."

"Of course."

Don Ambrosio again cleared his throat, smiled one last time, and looked ahead to the next group. In his mind he had already moved on.

"Good luck, Captain Alatriste."

"Good luck, Excellency."

The Marqués de los Balbases, Captain-General of Flanders, continued on. The path to glory and posterity lay before him—though he did not know it, and we were the ones who had to do all the hard work—through the magnum opus of Diego Velázquez, but it was also to be the pathway toward calumny and injustice dealt him by the adoptive country he had served so generously. Because while Spínola reaped victories for the king, who was ungrateful like all the kings the world has ever seen, enemies were cutting the ground from beneath his feet at court, far from the fields of battle, discrediting him before the monarch of languid gestures and pallid soul, who, good natured but weak, always managed to find himself where honorable wounds were being received. Instead of adorning himself in the appurtenances of war, this king dressed for palace balls, even the country dances Juan de Esquivel taught in his academy. Only five years after the time we are speaking of, the man who stormed Breda, the intelligent and expert military strategist, the man of courage who loved Spain to the point of sacrifice, was to die ill and disillusioned. Don Francisco de Quevedo would write a poem expressing Spain's loss.

> *You subjected the Palatinate,*
> *To benefit the Spanish monarchy.*
> *Your ideals countering their heresy.*

In Flanders we badly missed your gallantry,
E'en more In Italy . . . and now this eulogy,
amid sorrow we dare not contemplate.

As reward for his noble endeavors he received the standard wages our land of Cains—more stepmother than mother, ever base and miserly—holds for those who love her and serve her well: oblivion, the poison engendered by envy, ingratitude, and dishonor. And the greatest irony was that poor don Ambrosio would die with only an enemy to console him, Julio Mazarino, who, like him, was an Italian by birth, a future cardinal and minister of France, and the only person to comfort him on his deathbed. It was to him that our poor general would confess, with senile delirium: *"I die with neither honor nor reputation . . . They have taken everything from me, money, and honor . . . I was a decent man . . . This is not the payment forty years of service deserves."*

It was a few days after the mutiny had calmed that I became embroiled in a singular altercation. It happened the same day the pay was distributed, a day of leave granted our *tercio* before we returned to the Ooster canal. All Oudkerck was one great Spanish fiesta. Even the faces of the surly Flemish, whom only months before we had slashed and gored, cleared before the rain of gold that showered over the town. The presence of soldiers with full purses had the effect of producing, as if by magic, victuals that had previously been swallowed up by the earth. Beer and wine—the latter more appreciated by our troops, who, like the great Lope de Vega before them, called the former "ass piss"—flowed like water, and even the sun, warm overhead, helped brighten the party and shed its rays upon dancing in the streets, music, and card games. Houses with a sign on the front displaying swans or calabashes—I am referring to brothels and taverns, of course; in Spain we used branches of laurel or pine—were, as the old saying goes, making hay while the sun shines. Blonde, pale-skinned women recovered their hospitable smiles, and that day no few husbands, fathers, and brothers looked, more or less willingly, the other way while their women starched the tail of your shirt. There is no stone so hard that it cannot be softened by the timely clink of that pimp and procuress, gold. In addition, the Flemish women, liberal in their behavior and conversation, were not at all like our sanctimonious Spanish women. They willingly allowed you to take their hands and kiss them on the face, and it was not too great a challenge to strike up a friendship with one who claimed to be Catholic, evidenced by the fact that more than a few accompanied our soldiers on their return to Italy or Spain. Nevertheless, none was as perfect as Flora, the heroine of *El sitio de Bredá* (the Siege of Breda), whom the author, don Pedro Calderón de la Barca, undoubtedly exaggerating a little, endowed with laudable virtues: a Spanish sense of honor and a love for Spaniards that I never came across in any Flemish woman. Nor, I suspect, did Calderón.

But back to my story. I was telling Your Mercies that there in Oudkerk, the usual entourage of troops on campaign—soldiers' wives, whores, sutlers, gamblers, and people of every ilk—had set up their stalls outside of town, and soldiers were coming and going between these attractions and the town, dressing up threadbare duds with new trifles, plumes on hats, and other fripperies—as the sacristan knows, easy come, easy goes. There was wanton disregard of the Ten Commandments, and few theological or cardinal virtues were left inviolate. It was, in short, what the Flemish call *kermesse* and we Spaniards *jolgorio*, a rowdy celebration. Or as the veterans put it, we could have been in Italy.

The happy-go-lucky youth in me took in everything that day, as youths will do. Along with Jaime Correas, I saw every sight from Micah to Mecca, and although I was not much of a drinker, I downed the precious grape along with everyone else, among other reasons, because drinking and gambling were what soldiers did, and there was no shortage of acquaintances who offered me a quaff free of charge. As for gaming, I did none of that because we *mochileros* had no pay to collect, past or current, so I had naught to play with. But I stood around watching the circles of soldiers gathered round the drumheads they used for throwing dice and playing cards. For if most of the *miles gloriosus* among our men were strangers to the Ten Commandments and scarcely knew how to read or write, had writing been based on the markings of a pack of cards, everyone would have been as familiar with the book of prayer as they were with their deck of forty-eight.

Fair dice and loaded dice rolled across drumheads, and cards were as handily shuffled as if the action were taking place in the Potro square in Córdoba or the Patio de los Naranjos in Seville. There were numerous card games where players could throw in their money, among them *rentoy, manilla, quínolas,* and *pintas.* The center of the camp was one enormous gaming house, with "I'm in" and "I'm out," and more swearing than artillery fire, with a "Damn that whore of gold" here and an "It's your play" there, and not least a "'Fore God and your blessed mother." Those who talk loudest in such moments are the ones who, in battle, show more fear than iron in their spine but who make a great show of courage in the rear guard and who who wield the swords on cards faster than they unsheathe their own. One soldier gambled away the six months of pay that had been his reason to mutiny, losing it through blows of fate as mortal as any dagger. In fact, such blows were not always metaphorical; from time to time cheating would be revealed—a shaved card, a pin-pricked king, a die weighted with quicksilver—and then the air thickened with " 'Pon my life" and " 'Pon *your* life," "You lie through your teeth," and worse, followed by a downpour of blows as daggers cut, swords slashed, and blood was spilled that had nothing to do with the barber or with the art of Hippocrates.

What rabble is this? What men, what breeds?
Soldiers, Spaniards, plumes, and finery,
words, wit, lies, and gallantry,
Arrogance, bravura, and foul deeds.

I have already told Your Mercies that it was during this time that my virtue, like many other things, was carried off on the winds of Flanders. And in that regard I ended that day visiting, with Jaime Correas, a wheeled conveyance sheltered beneath a canvas and some boards where a certain *pater brothelia*, a pious enough calling where there is want, offered three or four of his parishioners to assuage manly woes.

There are six or seven varieties
of women, Otón, who sin,
all of them strolling along these shores,
shall we gather one in?

One of those "varieties" was a flamboyantly robed girl, fair of mien and limb and of a reasonable age, and my comrade and I had invested a good part of the booty we had harvested during the sacking of Oudkerk in her company. We had no jingling purse that day, but the girl, half Spanish, half Italian, a wench who called herself Clara de Mendoza—I never met a trollop who did not boast of being a de Mendoza or de Guzmán though she came from a line of swineherds—had looked on us with favorable eyes for some reason that escapes me, unless it was the insolence of our years and perhaps her belief that she who takes a young and grateful youth as a client will keep him all her life. At the end of the day we went down to her neck of the woods, more to look than with coins to spend. The vivacious Mendoza, though she was occupied in activities proper to her office, nonetheless sent a friendly word our way, along with a dazzling, if somewhat snaggle-toothed, smile. A certain loudmouthed soldier who was consorting with her at that moment did not take kindly to this. He was a fellow from Valencia, with a chestnut mustache and villainous beard, a burly, pugnacious type, and with his "Be off with you, forsooth!" he added a kick for my comrade and a slap for me, apportioning us equal shares. The punch to my cheek was more painful to my honor than to my face, and my youthful spirit, which a quasi-military life had not made more tolerant when confronted with such nonsense, duly responded. My right hand, of its own accord, went to the belt where my good Toledo dagger was snugged against my kidneys.

"Appreciate, Your Mercy," I said, "the disparity between our persons."

I did not actually pull my weapon, but the move was natural to someone born in Oñate, as I had been. As for the "disparity," I was referring to my being a young *mochilero* and he a lordly soldier, but this contentious fellow took my words for an insult, thinking that I was questioning his worth. The truth is, the presence of witnesses rubbed this blusterer up the wrong way, and he was also loaded to the gills, for sloshing around in his innards was a great quantity of wine, as his breath betrayed. But without further preamble, the words were scarcely out of my mouth, before he came at me like a madman, putting hand to his storied weapon, Durendal. People jumped aside, and not one soul intervened, apparently believing that I was lad enough to back my words with action. May God send down his thunderbolts on those who left me in that pickle. How cruel is the human condition when there is a spectacle to be witnessed, for not one of those bystanders aspired to make redemption his vocation, and I, who at that point in the proceedings could not put my tongue back into its scabbard, had no recourse but to pull out my dagger, hoping to make the game a little more even-handed, or at least to avoid ending my soldierly career like a chicken on a spit.

Life in the service of Captain Alatriste and the army in Flanders had taught me a certain cunning, and I was a vigorous lad of fairly good size. And besides, La Mendoza was watching. So I stepped back from the sword tip, squarely facing the Valencian, who, completely at ease, began to make passes at me with the sharp edges of his sword, the kind of moves that do not kill but that make you happy to leave the scene. I could not run away, however—there was my reputation to consider—and I could not stand fast because of the discrepancy between our blades. I was tempted to throw my dagger at him, but I kept a cool head, despite my foreboding; I was aware that the final curtain would come down if I missed. My opponent kept coming at me with all the tricks of a Turk, and I kept moving back, well aware that I was inferior in weapons, body, strength, and expertise: He had his Toledo blade, was strong as an ox when sober, and skilled, whereas I was a wet-behind-the-ears youth with a dagger and bravado that would not serve me as shield. I envisioned that at least a split head—mine—would be the booty from this campaign.

"Com'ere, then, young capon," the fellow said.

As he spoke, the wine in his belly caused him to stumble, so without his having to ask twice, I did as he requested. And as with the agility of my young years I was able to dodge his steel, covering my face with my left arm in case he should cut me off midway, I slashed with my dagger: right to left, above and below. Had it been a little longer, that blade would have left the king without a soldier and Valencia without a favorite son. To my good fortune, I jumped clear without major injury, but having only scratched my adversary's groin—which is where I had aimed my thrust—severing his trouser latchet and drawing a "God's Blood!" that brought laughter from the witnesses and also some applause that, though little consolation, indicated that the crowd was on my side.

My attack, I can safely say, was a mistake, for everyone had seen that I was not some poor defenseless little boy, and now no one would step in or even plan to step in. Even my comrade, Jaime Correas, was urging me on, delighted with my performance in the altercation. The worst part was that with my blow the wine fumes that had befogged my opponent suddenly dissipated; with renewed vigor, he was now ready to make mincemeat of me. Horrified at the thought of going to my reward without confessing but with little choice, I resolved to make a second and final move: I would slip between the Valencian's sword and his belly, stay in there somehow, and stab and stab and stab until one of the two of us was sent off with a letter for the devil. Lacking absolution and last rites, I would manufacture the necessary explanations. Strangely, years later a

French author would write: "A Spaniard, having determined the move he will make with his knife, will carry
through though he be cut to pieces," and when I read that,
I thought that nothing could better express the decision I
had made confronting the Valencian. I took a deep breath,
gritted my teeth, and as my enemy took one of the two-
handed swings he was directing at me, I awaited the moment when the tip of his sword reached the point of the
arc farthest from me, and planned to lunge at him with my
dagger. And I would have done it, *pardiez*, had powerful
hands not grabbed me by an arm and the nape of the neck
at the same time a body stepped between me and my
enemy. I looked up, dumbfounded, to meet the cold gray-
green eyes of Captain Alatriste.

"The boy was not much of a match for a brave man
like you."

The scene had shifted, and now the action was being
played out beside the canal and with relative discretion.
Diego Alatriste and the Valencian were some fifty strides
from the original site, at the foot of the embankment of a
dike that hid them from the camp. Up on the dike, con-
siderably higher above them, my master's friends were
keeping away the curious. They were very casual about it
but nevertheless formed a barrier that prevented anyone

from passing. Llop, Rivas, Mendieta were there and a few others, including Sebastián Copons. It was the latter's iron hands that had plucked me from my imbroglio, and now I was standing beside him, watching what was happening below on the shore of the canal. All around me Alatriste's friends were acting nonchalant, gazing off in different directions, discouraging anyone attempting to come take a look with fierce glances, twisting of mustaches, and hands poised on the pommels of swords. So that everything would be conducted in the proper manner, they had brought along two of the Valencian's acquaintances in case witnesses should be needed regarding the settling of affairs.

"You would never," Alatriste added, "want to be called a baby butcher."

He said it with ice and derision in his voice, and in return the Valencian growled a blasphemous curse. There was no trace of the vapors of wine left in him, and he was running his left hand over his beard and mustache, piqued, still holding his unsheathed weapon in his right hand. Despite his menacing appearance and the threat of the naked blade, one could read between the lines that he was not entirely inclined toward swordplay, otherwise he would already have launched his attack against the captain, resolved to get in the first thrust. Pride and concern for his reputation had brought him here, along with the questionable state of his honor after his encounter with me, but from time to time he glanced up toward the top of the embankment, as if he still trusted that someone would step in before the matter went any further. The primary focus of his attention, however, was on the movements of Diego Alatriste, who very slowly, as if he had all the time in the world, had taken off his hat, then, with measured movements, had pulled the bandolier with the twelve apostles over his head and laid it and his harquebus on the ground near the canal. Now, cool and collected, he was unfastening his doublet.

"A brave man like you," Alatriste repeated, his eyes locked with the Valencian's.

The second time the captain had uttered that *como vos*, "like you," with such cold sarcasm, the Valencian had snorted with fury, looked up at the men on the embankment, taken one step forward and another to the side, and whipped his sword back and forth. When not used among good acquaintances, friends, or persons of very different status, that *vos* rather than *uced* or "Your Mercy," was not very courteous and was often considered an insult by the invariably thin-skinned Spaniard. If we consider that in Naples the Conde de Lemos and don Juan de Zúñiga took out their swords—they and all their retinue, even their servants—and that one hundred and fifty blades were drawn that day because one called the other *señoría* instead of "excellency" and because the other returned with *vuesamerced* instead of *señoría*, it is easy to judge the extent of such sensitivities. It was painstakingly clear that the Valencian could not willingly endure that *vos*, and that despite his indecision—it was evident that he knew the man standing before him by sight and reputation—he was left with no option but to fight. To sheathe his sword before another soldier who had addressed him as *vos*, especially as he was brandishing his sword with such swagger, would have been a black mark on his reputation.

In Spanish, the word *reputation* was, in those days, a very weighty word. Not for nothing had we Spaniards fought for a century and a half in Europe, ruining ourselves to defend the true religion and our reputation, while the Lutherans, Calvinists, Anglicans, and other accursed heretics, despite spicing their stew with a lot of Bible and freedom of thought, had fought so that their merchants and their companies in the Indies could earn more money. Reputation was of little concern to them if it did not offer practical advantages. It has always been our way, however, to be guided less by practical sense than by the *ora-pro-nobis* and the "what-will-people-say"? So that was how things were in Europe, and that is how things were with us.

"No one invited you to bring your candle to this funeral," the Valencian said hoarsely.

"True," Alatriste conceded, as if he had thought carefully about candles and funerals, "but I thought that a fine soldier like *you*—again that *vos*—deserved someone who was more your own size, so I hope to be of service."

By now Alatriste was in his shirtsleeves, and the stitched tears, patched hose, and old boots tied below the knee with harquebus cord did not diminish his imposing appearance one whit. The water in the canal reflected the gleam of his sword as he drew it from the scabbard.

"If it please you, would you tell me your name?"

The Valencian, who was unfastening a jerkin with as many rips and tears as the captain's shirt, gave a surly nod. His eyes never left his adversary's blade.

"My name is García de Candau."

"A pleasure." Alatriste had put his left hand behind him, and in it now glinted the Vizcaína, his dagger with the shepherd's crook guards. "Mine . . . "

"I know what you are," the other interrupted. "You are that charlatan captain who gives himself a title he does not possess."

Atop the embankment, Alatriste's men looked at each other. The wine had given the Valencian some nerve after all. Those familiar with Diego Alatriste knew that if the man were hoping to get out of this with nothing more than a wound or two and a few weeks on his back, wading into those deep waters was a fatal card to play. We all watched expectantly, determined not to lose a single moment.

Then I saw that Diego Alatriste was smiling. I had lived

with him long enough to know that smile: a grimace beneath his mustache, a funereal omen bloodthirsty as a weary wolf once again preparing for the kill but without passion and without hunger, simply doing its job.

As they pulled the Valencian onto land, blood stained the calm waters of the canal around him. Everything had been done in accord with the rules of fencing and of decency, man to man, feet set, swords slashing, daggers playing, until Captain Alatriste's blade entered where it was wont. And when questions arose about that death—amid cards, quarrels, and slaughtering knives, three others were dispatched that day, along with half a dozen wounded—the witnesses, all soldiers of our lord and king, and men whose word was trusted, said straight out that the Valencian had fallen into the canal after drinking himself senseless, wounding himself with his own weapon. So the chief bailiff of the *tercio*, privately relieved, declared the matter closed and bade everyone to go tend his roses. As if that wasn't enough, that very night the Dutch attacked. And the bailiff, the colonel, the soldiers, Captain Alatriste and I as well, had—God knows it—more urgent things to think about.

5. THE LOYAL INFANTRY

The enemy attacked in the middle of the night, and the men at the "forlorn hope" postings were precisely that, without hope, slaughtered without even the time to flick an eyelash. Informed by his spies, Maurice of Nassau had seized the opportunity offered by the churning waters of the mutiny. Planning to install a relief unit of Dutch and English troops in Breda, he had approached Oudkerk from the north with large numbers of infantry and cavalry, and in their progress they had wreaked havoc and destruction at our advance posts. The Cartagena *tercio*, along with Don Carlos Soest's Walloon infantry detachment, which was camped nearby, received the order to intercept the Hollanders and hold them back until our General Spínola could organize the counterattack. So in the middle of the night we were routed from sleep by drums and fifes and calls to collect our weapons. No one who has not lived such moments can imagine the clamor and confusion: lit torches illuminating running, pushing, startled figures, their faces serene, grave, terrorized. There were contradictory orders, captains shouting, sergeants hastily lining up rows of half-asleep, half-dressed soldiers and trying to get them outfitted for battle. All this chaos played out against the deafening *rat-a-tat-tat* of drums from the camp to the town, people scrambling to their windows and up on the walls, camps being struck, whinnying horses maddened by hands conveying the threat of combat. Battle-torn banners were drawn from their sheaths and unfurled to ripple in the breeze: crosses of Burgundy, bars of Aragon, quarters with castles and lions and chains, all rippling in the red light of torches and bonfires.

Captain Bragado's company was among the first to march off, leaving behind the fires of the fortified town and camp and plunging into darkness along a dike bordering vast salt marshes and peat bogs. The word ran down the line of soldiers that we were marching to the Ruyter mill, a place the Dutch would have to pass en route to Breda because the land was narrow there, and according to what we'd been told, it was not possible to ford the river anywhere else. I was walking with the other *mochileros* from Diego Alatriste's company, carrying his and Sebastián Copons's harquebuses. I stayed close behind them, for I was also carrying a store of powder and balls and part of their supplies. Despite the dubious privilege of being loaded like a mule, this daily exercise had the benefit of strengthening my arms and legs. We Spaniards always do find a way to shrug off our troubles: From every ill some good will come, or vice versa.

Well, my brothers and señores,
you know without my explanation
an honor is never, ever, won
except with extreme extenuation.

The march was not easy in that murky light, for the moon was new and almost always hidden behind the clouds, so now and again some soldier would stumble, or the line would stop and you would bump into the person ahead of you, and then all along the dike the " 'Pon my lifes" and *"Pardiezes"* erupted like a hailstorm of shot. My master was, as usual, a silent silhouette I followed like the shadow of a shadow. As we walked along, my head and my heart were filled with conflicting emotions: on one hand, a youth's normal excitement about imminent action, but on the other, misgivings about the darkness and the prospect of battling a substantial number of enemies on open ground. Perhaps that was why it had made such an impression on me when, still in Oudkerk and just as the *tercio* had fallen in by the torchlight, even the most vocal nonbelievers had taken a moment to kneel and bare their heads as Chaplain Salanueva went up and down the rows giving us general absolution, just in case. For although the padre was a sullen and stupid priest who in his cups always tangled his Latin, he was, after all, the closest thing to a holy man we had. In any case, one thing does not cancel the other, and in a bad situation our soldiers always preferred an *ego te absolvo* from a sinner's hand to heading toward the next world with nothing to cover their sins.

One detail disturbed me greatly, however, and from the comments I heard around me, the veteran soldiers had also given it some thought. As we crossed one of the bridges near the dike, we saw by the light of some lanterns that sappers—those entrusted with disarming the mines—with axes and mattocks were preparing to tear down the bridge behind us, no doubt to deprive the Dutch of a passage through that area. However, that also meant that we ourselves could not expect reinforcements from the rear. And also, if it eventually came to "every man for himself," it would be impossible to retreat in that direction. There were other bridges, no doubt, but imagine, Your Mercies, the effect that had on us as we marched toward the enemy in that black night.

Nevertheless, with or without a bridge behind us, we

reached the Ruyter mill before dawn. From there you could hear the distant bursts of shots as our most advanced harquebusiers kept the Dutch entertained. A bonfire was burning, and in its splendor we could see the miller and his family, a woman and four very young children, all frightened and in their nightclothes, who had been driven from their home and were watching, powerless, as soldiers broke down doors and windows, fortified the upper floor, and piled up demolished furnishings to form a bulwark. As the flames reflected off helmets and corselets, the children sobbed from terror of those rough men clad in steel, and the miller held his head in his hands, watching as his livelihood was ruined, his property devastated, and no one was moved in the least by his fate. In war, tragedy becomes routine, and the soldier's heart is hardened as much by the misfortune of others as by his own. As for the mill, our colonel had chosen it as a lookout and command post, and we could see don Pedro de la Daga in the doorway, conferring with the Walloon commander, each surrounded by his principal officers and flag bearers. From time to time they turned to look toward the distant fires a half league or so away as well as the hamlets burning in the distance, where the main body of the Dutch seemed to be concentrated.

We were made to march on a little farther, leaving the mill behind, and the companies spread out in the darkness among the hedgerows and beneath the trees, walking through tall wet grass that soaked us to the knees. The order was not to light fires and to wait. Occasionally a nearby shot or a false alarm sent a shudder through our lines, evoking a burst of "Halt!" and "Who goes there?" Fear and watchfulness are bad companions to repose. The men in the vanguard were keeping their harquebus cords lit, and in the dark the red tips glowed like fireflies. The real veterans dropped to the wet ground right there, determined to rest before the battle. Others chose not to or were unable, and were wide awake, alert, their eyes staring into the night, attentive to the sporadic fire of the advance scouts skirmishing nearby.

As for me, I kept as close as I could to Captain Alatriste, who, with the rest of his squad, had gone to lie down by a hedgerow. I followed them, feeling my way, and had the bad luck to run into a patch of brambles that tore at my face and hands. Twice I heard my master's voice calling me to make sure I was keeping up. Finally he and Sebastián asked for their harquebuses, and they charged me with keeping a cord lit at both ends in case they needed it. So I took my steel and flint from my pack, and in the shelter of the hedge I struck my spark and did what they had ordered me to do. I blew hard on the slow match and hung it on a stick I set in the ground so it would stay dry and lit. Then I curled up with everyone else, trying to rest from the march and perhaps sleep a little. It was no use; it was too cold. Beneath me the wet grass soaked my clothing, and from above, the night dew drenched us thoroughly as if Beelzebub himself had ordered it. Scarcely aware, I pushed closer to the warmth of Diego Alatriste, who lay stretched out with his harquebus tucked between his legs. I could smell the odor of dirty clothes mixed with traces of leather and metal, and pushed closer still, seeking warmth. He did not discourage me but lay absolutely still when he felt me near. Only later, when the coming dawn streaked the sky and I began to shiver, did he turn over an instant and without a word cover me with his old soldier's cape.

The Hollanders appeared, capable and confident, with the first rays of the sun. Their light cavalry scattered our advance harquebusiers, and in no time they were upon us in close, orderly rows, their aim to take control of the Ruyter mill and the road that led through Oudkerk to Breda. Captain Bragado's *bandera* was ordered to form up with the rest of the *tercio* in a hedge-and-tree-bordered meadow between the marsh and the road. The Walloon infantry of don Carlos Soest—all Flemish Catholics are loyal to our lord and king—lined up on the other side of the road so that between our two *tercios* we covered a strip a quarter of a league wide through which the Dutch would have to pass. And by my faith, it was an admirable and noble sight, those two *tercios* stationed in the middle of the meadows with banners flying above a forest of pikes and detachments of harquebuses and muskets covering the front and the flanks, while the gentle roll of the land atop the nearby dikes was filled with the advancing enemy. That day we were going to be one against five; it almost seemed as if Maurice of Nassau had emptied the Estates of inhabitants in order to throw every one of them against us.

"By heaven, this does not augur well," I heard Captain Bragado say.

"At least they don't have artillery," Lieutenant Coto, the standard bearer, pointed out.

"At the moment."

With eyes squinting beneath the brims of their hats, they, like the rest of us Spaniards, were making a professional assessment of the glinting pikes, breastplates, and helmets that were beginning to blot out the landscape that spread before the Cartagena *tercio*. Diego Alatriste's squad was at the forefront, harquebuses at the ready, their muskets resting in forks, musket balls in mouths, ready to be spat into barrels, and cords lit at both ends, forming a protective shield for the left wing of the *tercio* and aligned in front of the *picas secas* and *coseletes* who stood only half an arm's length from the next. The former had only their pikes as protection while the latter were armored in helmet, gorget, and cuirasses, and waited with their sixteen-foot-long pikes rammed into the ground.

I was within earshot of Captain Alatriste, ready to provide him and his comrades with powder, one-ounce lead shot, and water when they had need of it. My eyes traveled back and forth between the ever-thicker rows of Dutchmen and the expressionless faces of my master and his comrades, who were standing motionless in their positions. There was no conversation among them other than an occasional comment spoken quietly to the nearest companion, an appraising look here and there, a silently mouthed orison, a twist of a mustache, or a tongue run over dry lips. Waiting. Excited by the imminent combat and wanting to be useful, I went over to Captain Alatriste to see if he needed a drink or if there was anything I could bring him, but he scarcely took note of me. He was holding his harquebus by the barrel, with the butt set on the ground, and he had a smoldering cord wrapped around his left wrist, while he intently observed the enemy field with his gray-green eyes. The brim of his hat shaded his face, and his buffcoat was tightly wrapped beneath the bandolier with the twelve apostles and the belt with sword, *vizcaína*, and powder flask strapped over a faded red band. The aquiline profile dramatized by the enormous mustache, the tanned skin of his face, and the sunken cheeks unshaved since the previous day made him look even leaner than usual.

"Eyes left!" Bragado alerted them, snapping his captain's short lance to his shoulder.

On our left, between the peat bogs and the nearby trees, several Dutch horsemen were reconnoitering, exploring the lay of the land. Without awaiting orders, Garrote, Llop, and four or five harquebusiers stepped forward a few paces, poured a bit of loose powder into their pans, and, aiming carefully, fired off shots in the direction of the heretics, who pulled up on their reins and retired without further ado. Across the road, the enemy had already reached Soest's *tercio* and were battering them at close range with harquebus fire. The Walloons were firing back, shot for shot. I watched as a large company of horse approached with the intention of charging and saw the Walloon pikes tilt forward like a shimmering grove of ash wood and steel, ready to welcome them.

"Here they come," said Bragado.

Lieutenant Coto, who was armored in a cuirass with chain-mail sleeves—in his role as standard bearer he was exposed to enemy fire and all manner of enemy aggression —took the banner from the hands of his second lieutenant and went to join the other banners in the center of the *tercio*. Outlined before us by the first horizontal rays of the sun, the Dutch were approaching in their hundreds, re-forming their lines through trees and hedges as they came out into the meadow. They were yelling and shouting to keep up their courage, and the many Englishmen with them were as vociferous in fighting as they were in drinking. Still advancing, they lined up in perfect formation two hundred paces away, their harquebusiers already firing at us, though we were out of range.

I have already told Your Mercies, I believe, that despite my experience in Flanders, this was my first combat in open country, and never until then had I witnessed Spaniards steadfastly standing their ground in the face of an attack. What was most memorable was the silence in which they waited, the absolute fixity with which those rows of dark-skinned, bearded men from the most undisciplined land on earth watched the enemy approach with ne'er a word, a flinch, a gesture that had not been regulated in accord with the commands of our lord and king. It was that day, there at the Ruyter mill that I truly came to understand why our infantry was, and for so long had been, the most feared in all of Europe. The *tercio* was a faultless, disciplined military machine in which each soldier knew his role; that was their strength and their pride. For those men, a motley army composed of hidalgos, adventurers, and the ruffians and dregs of all the Spains, to fight honorably for the Catholic monarchy and for the true religion conferred on any who did so, even the lowest of the low, a dignity impossible to achieve in any other way.

I left my land to fight in Flanders,
Where, though not first-born nor heir,
younger sons, by being soldiers
achieved in war what had not been theirs.

The prolific genius of Toledo, *fray* Gabriel Téllez, known by the more famous name of Tirso de Molina, wrote very knowingly on this subject. By basking in the unassailable reputation of the *tercios*, even the basest scallywag had reason to call himself an hidalgo.

My lineage begins with me,
for those men are better still
who institute their ancestry;
worse are those who would defame
what once had been an honored name.

As for the Dutch, they did not waste time putting on such airs, and they did not give a spoiled herring for bloodlines. No, that morning they were headed straight for Breda, valiant, determined to take the shortest route. A few of their muskets were already smoking, having propelled lead balls to the limit of their reach, where they rolled harmlessly across the grass. I saw our *maestre* don Pedro de la Daga, on his mount beside the standard bearers and heavily armored in Milanese iron, lower the sallet of his helmet with one hand and lift his baton of command with the other. With that, the lead drum sounded, and immediately all the others joined in. That drumming went on forever, and it seemed to have frozen everyone's blood because a mortal silence fell over the field. The Dutch, so close now we could see their faces, also paused for an instant, hesitating, affected by the drumbeat issuing from the motionless lines blocking their passage. Then, whipped up by their corporals and officers, they resumed their advance, shouting as they came. By now they were very close, some sixty or seventy paces, with pikes at the ready and harquebuses aimed.

Then a cry began to ripple through the *tercio*, a harsh defiant shout repeated from line to line, rising in a clamor that drowned out the sound rolling off the drumheads:

"Spain! . . . Spain! . . . Close in for Spain!"

That *Close in!* was an old battle cry, and it always meant one thing: Watch out; Spain is on the attack. When I heard it, I caught my breath and turned to look at Diego Alatriste, but I couldn't tell whether he had yelled the phrase or not. The first rows of Spaniards were moving forward to the beat of the drums, and the captain was advancing with them, his harquebus loose in his hands, elbow to elbow with his comrades: Sebastián Copons on one side and Mendieta on the other, tight to Captain Bragado's side and leaving no spaces between them. The entire *tercio* was marching at the same slow, orderly, proud pace as though they were on parade before the king. Only a few days before, many of these same men had mutinied over unpaid wages, but now they were soldiers: teeth clenched, mustaches and beards bristling, their rags covered by cuirasses of oiled leather, and their weapons polished, they fixed their eyes on the enemy, an intrepid, terrible force that trailed the smoke of lit harquebus cords. I ran behind, not wanting to lose sight of the captain, through heretic fire that was truly raining down on us now that their *coseletes* and harquebusiers were well within range. I was breathless, deafened by the roar of my own blood, which was pounding in my veins and eardrums as if the *tercio*'s drums were reverberating in my innards.

The Hollanders' first round took down one of our men and enveloped us all in a cloud of smoke. When that dissipated I saw Captain Bragado with his captain's lance upraised: Alatriste and his comrades had stopped, and with complete calm they had blown on their cords and positioned their harquebuses to their cheeks to take aim. And so, in battle mode, some thirty paces from the Hollanders, the old Cartagena *tercio* entered the fray.

"Close ranks! . . . Close ranks!"

There had been sun in the sky for two hours, and the *tercio* had been fighting since dawn. The forward lines of Spanish harquebusiers had held their ground, inflicting considerable damage to the Dutch until, harassed by musket balls and pikes and skirmishes with cavalry, they disengaged, never turning their backs to the enemy as they moved back to join the *tercio* where, along with the pike men, they formed an impenetrable wall. With each charge, each round of fire, the empty spaces left by fallen men were filled by those still standing, and each time the Hollanders attempted to approach, they encountered a barrier of pikes and muskets that had already driven them back twice.

"And here they come again!"

You would have said that the devil was vomiting heretics, for this was the third time they had charged us. Their lances were close upon us again, the pike tips gleaming through the thick smoke. Our officers were hoarse from shouting orders; Captain Bragado had lost his hat in the fracas, and his face was black with gunpowder, but the Dutch blood on his blade ran red and had never had time to dry.

"Pikes at the ready!"

In the forward lines of the squad, less than a foot apart and well protected in their breastplates and helmets of copper and steel, the *coseletes* took up their long pikes. After rocking the pike in his left hand, the coselete would grasp it with his right and bring it to a horizontal position, ready to trade thrusts with the enemy. Meanwhile, our harquebusiers along the flanks were making serious inroads among the Dutch. I found myself in the midst of them, keeping close to my master's squad and trying not to get in the way of the men who were loading and shooting. I ran back and forth, bringing this person a supply of powder, that one lead balls, handing another the flask of water I had tied to my bandolier. All the smoke from the muskets hampered both my vision and my sense of smell, filling my eyes with tears. Most of the time I had to fight my way almost blindly among the men who were shouting for me.

I had just delivered a handful of balls to Captain Alatriste, who was running short. I watched as he dropped several into the pouch he wore hanging over his right thigh, put two in his mouth and another into the muzzle of the harquebus, rammed it home, and then poured loose powder into the pan. He then blew on the cord rolled around his left wrist, placed it in the hammer of the lock, and raised the weapon to his cheek to aim at the nearest Hollander. He performed all those actions almost unconsciously, never taking his eyes from his target, and when the shot sped away I saw a hole open in the iron breastplate of a pike man wearing an enormous helmet and the heretic fall backward, disappearing among his comrades.

To our right, pikes clashed with the pikes of heretic *coseletes* who had joined the attack on us. Diego Alatriste leaned over the hot barrel of his harquebus, spat a ball into the muzzle, coolly repeated his routine, and fired. Traces of his own burned powder covered his face and mustache with gray, making him seem older. His eyes, reddened and encircled with powder residue that accentuated his wrinkles, focused with obstinate concentration on the advance of the Dutch lines, and when he picked out a new target to aim at, he watched his mark as if he feared he would fade from sight, as if killing him and no other were a personal matter. I had the impression that he chose his prey with great care.

"They are here!" shouted Captain Bragado. "Hold! . . . Hold fast!"

To do that, to hold, God and the king had given Bragado two hands, a sword, and a hundred Spaniards, and it was time to use them to the fullest, because Dutch pikes were coming toward us with lethal intent. Through the roar of shots I heard Mendieta curse with that fervor we Basques are capable of, because the lock of his harquebus had been sheared off. At that moment a lead sparrow flew past my ear, *whirrr . . . pock*, and a soldier close behind me went down. On our right the landscape was a forest of entangled Spanish and Dutch pikes, and, with an undulation of steel, part of that line, too, was swinging around to engage us. I saw Mendieta whip his harquebus over and grab it by the barrel to use it as a club. Everyone hastily discharged his last ball.

"Spain! . . . Santiago! . . . Spain!"

At our backs, behind the pikes, rippled the shot-shredded crosses of St. Andrew. The Hollanders were right upon us, an avalanche of frightened or terrible eyes and blood-covered faces. Large, blond, courageous heretics were attempting to bury their pikes and halberds in us or run us through with their swords. I watched as Alatriste and Copons, shoulder to shoulder, dropped their harquebuses to the ground and unsheathed their Toledo blades, planting their feet firmly. I also watched as Dutch pikes penetrated our lines, and saw their lances wound and mutilate, twisting in bloody flesh. Diego Alatriste was slashing with sword and dagger among the long ash pikes. I grabbed one as it went by me and a Spaniard beside me plunged his sword into the neck of the Hollander holding the far end; his blood streamed down the shaft onto my hands. Now Spanish pikes were coming to our aid, approaching from behind us to attack the Dutch over our backs and through the spaces left by the dead. Everything was a labyrinth of lances and a crescendo of carnage.

I fought my way toward Alatriste, pushing through our comrades. When a Hollander cut his way through our men with his sword and fell at the captain's feet, locking his arm around his legs with the intention of pulling him down as well, I gave a loud shout, pulled out my dagger, and sprang toward him, determined to defend my master, even if I was cut to pieces in the process. Blinded by my madness, I fell upon the heretic, flattened my hand over his face and pressed his head to the ground. Alatriste kicked and pulled to be free of him and twice plunged his sword into the man's body from above. The Hollander rolled over but was not yet willing to give up the ghost. He was a hearty man, but he was bleeding from his mouth and nose like a Jarama bull at the end of a corrida. I can remember the sticky feel of his blood—red and streaked with gunpowder—and the dirt and blond stubble on his white, freckled face. He fought me, unresigned to dying, whoreson that he was, and I fought him back. Still holding him down with my left hand, I tightened my grip on the dagger in my right and stabbed him three times in the ribs, but I was so close to his chest that all three attempts slid across the leather buffcoat protecting his torso. He felt the blows, for I saw his eyes open wide, and at last he released my master's legs in order to protect his face, as if he were afraid I would wound him there. He moaned. I was blinded by fear and fury, deranged by this mongrel, who so obstinately refused to die. I stuck the tip of the dagger between the fastenings of his buffcoat. *"Neee. . . . Srinden. . . . Nee,"* the heretic murmured, and I pressed down with all the weight of my body. In less than an Ave Maria he spat up one last vomit of blood, his eyes rolled back in his head, and he lay as still as if he had never had life.

"Spain! . . . They're pulling back! . . . Spaaaain!"

The battered rows of Dutch were withdrawing, treading heedlessly on the corpses of their comrades and leaving the grass seasoned with dead. A few inexperienced Spaniards made as if to pursue them, but the greater number of soldiers stayed where they were. As the men of the Cartagena *tercio* were nearly all old veterans, they were too practiced in war to break from their lines and risk a flank attack or an ambush. I felt Alatriste's hand grab the neck of my jerkin and turn me around to see whether I was hurt. When I looked up I saw only those gray-green eyes. Then without a further word or gesture, he yanked me right off my dead Dutchman, who was now nothing but cold meat. The arm that held his sword seemed to be almost too exhausted even to sheathe the blade he had wiped clean on the buffcoat of the dead man. He had blood on his face, on his hands, and on his clothing, but none of it was his. I looked around. Sebastián Copons, who was searching for his harquebus among a pile of Spanish and Dutch corpses was covered with his own, bleeding from a gaping wound on his temple.

"Zounds!" the Argonese blurted, dazed, feeling the two-inch flap of scalp hanging loose over his left ear.

He held the severed skin between a thumb and index finger blackened with blood and powder, not knowing quite what to do with it. Alatriste took a clean linen from his pouch and, after laying the skin back in place as best he could, knotted the cloth around Copons's head.

"Those blond toads almost got me, Diego."

"That will be another day."

Copons shrugged his shoulders. "Another day."

I stumbled to my feet; the soldiers were falling back into line, moving aside the fallen Dutch. Some seized the opportunity to search the corpses, divesting them of any valuables they found. I saw Garrote rather routinely using his *vizcaína* to cut off fingers, stuffing the rings they'd held into his pockets, and Mendieta was able to provide himself with a new harquebus.

"Close ranks!" bellowed Captain Bragado.

A hundred paces away, the Dutch reserves were forming up, and among them shone the breastplates of their cavalry. The Spanish soldiers temporarily put aside stripping bodies and again lined up elbow to elbow as the wounded crawled away, escaping the field however they could. We had to pull away our own dead to make room for the formation. The *tercio* had not yielded an inch of terrain.

That was our amusement for the morning, and we lasted till midday, taking the Hollanders' charges without giving way, calling out "Santiago!" and "Spain!" as they came toward us. We removed our dead and bandaged our wounded where they had fallen, until the heretics, convinced that this wall of dispassionate men did not intend to budge one inch, began to attack with less enthusiasm. My supplies of powder and musket balls had run dry, and I had turned to requisitioning them from corpses. At times, between attacks when the Dutch were farthest away, I would run a good distance out onto open ground and strip what I needed from their fallen harquebusiers, and more than once I had to come running back like a hare with their musket balls whirring past my ears. I had also used up the water I had brought for my master and his comrades—war raises a devilish thirst—and I made trip after trip to the canal at our backs. That was not a pleasant excursion because I had to pick my way among the wounded and dead we had dragged there, a blood-chilling panorama of appalling mutilations, bleeding stumps, laments in all the tongues of Spain, death rattles, prayers, blasphemies, and Salanueva's limping Latin as he went back and forth among the soldiers, his hand weary from administering extreme unctions which, once the oils were exhausted, he gave using only saliva. These fools who prate of the glory of war and majesty of battle should remember the words of the Marqués de Pescara: "May God grant me one hundred years of war and not one day of battle." They should walk where I walked that morning if they are truly to know the scene: the spectacular stage machinery of banners and bugles, the tall tales invented by the braggarts of the rear guard, the ones whose profiles adorn coins and who are immortalized in statues though they have never heard a shot whistling past their ears, or seen their comrades die, or stained their hands with the blood of an enemy, or run the risk of having their tackle blown off by a musket ball to the groin.

I used the trips back and forth to the canal to take a quick look at the road from the Ruyter mill and Oudkerk to see if help was on the way, but it was always empty. From there I could also see the whole of the field of battle, with the Dutch pushing toward us and our two *tercios* blocking passage on both sides of the road; Spaniards on my left and Soest's contingent on the right: an infinity of glinting steel, musket fire, gunpowder smoke, and banners amid a thick forest of pikes. Our Walloon comrades were playing their part well, and theirs, it is true, was the most difficult, squeezed as they were between the heretics' harquebusiers and brutal charges of Light Horse. Each time they held against a new assault there were fewer pikes in their squad, and although Soest's soldiers were men of great honor and integrity, they were inevitably losing strength. The danger was that if they gave way, the Dutch would be able to cross their terrain, flank the Cartagena *tercio*, and gain the advantage. And the Ruyter mill and road to Oudkerk and Breda would be lost.

I went back to my own company with those thoughts playing uneasily on my mind, and I was not encouraged when I passed by our colonel, who was positioned with other mounted officers in the middle of the squad. His armor had stopped a Dutch musket ball, though it had already traveled such a long distance that it left only a fine dent in his tooled Milanese steel breastplate. Except for that, our colonel seemed in good health, unlike his bugler, who had been shot in the mouth and now lay on the ground at his horse's hooves, with no one giving a fig whether he was bugling or not. I saw that don Pedro de la Daga and his cadre of officers were observing the Walloons' badly compromised lines with furrowed brows. Even I, inexperienced as I was, understood that if Soest's *tercio* collapsed, we Spaniards, with no cavalry to shield us, would have no recourse but to retreat to the Ruyter mill if we were to avoid being flanked. The ruinous effect would be that when the Dutch saw the *tercio* retreat, they would move on toward Breda. The respect and fear an enemy entertains when it encounters a wall of resolute men is very different from its attitude when it perceives that those men are looking less for a quarrel than for their own continued good health, and even more so at a time when we Spaniards were as renowned for our cruelty in attacking as we were for our pride and imperturbability in the face of death. Until then almost no one had seen the color of our backs, not even on canvas, and our pikes and our reputations were equally esteemed.

The sun was reaching its zenith when the Walloons, having served their king and the true religion with great dignity, finally collapsed. A charge of horse and the pressure of the Dutch infantry finally shredded their lines, and from our side of the road we watched as, despite the efforts of their officers, one section of troops withdrew toward the Ruyter mill and the other, more complete, surged toward us, seeking refuge in our formation. With them, surrounded by officers trying to save the standards, came their maestre, don Carlos Soest, like a condemned man, with his helmet missing and both arms broken by harquebus fire. They rushed toward us in such disorder that they nearly broke up our *tercio*. Even worse, however, was that right behind them, almost within reach, came the Hollander Horse and Foot, eager to accomplish their task by wiping out two regiments in one fell swoop. To our good fortune, they came straight from their first assault—their lines were ragged, and they were testing their luck to see whether we would come apart in all the confusion—but as I have said, the men of the Cartagena *tercio* were battle-wise and had seen everything. Almost without receiving orders, after allowing a reasonable number of Walloons to pass, the lines of our right flank closed as if they were made of iron, and harquebuses and muskets loosed an awesome round of fire that dispatched—two for the price of one—a good portion of the tag ends of Soest's *tercio* along with the Hollanders pursuing them from the rear.

"Pikes to the right!"

Without hurrying and with the sangfroid their legendary discipline implied, the rows of *coseletes* on our flank veered to face the Dutch. They drove the butt end of their pikes into the ground, firmed the mud around it with a foot, and pointed the blade end to the front, holding the shaft in their left hands as they unsheathed their swords with their right, preparing to cripple the horses racing toward them.

"Santiago! . . . Spain and Santiago!"

It was as if the Dutch had hit a solid brick wall. The collision with our right flank was so brutal that long pike shafts buried in the horses broke into pieces, and defenders and attackers were entangled in a muddle of lances, swords, daggers, knives, and harquebuses-turned-clubs.

"Pikes to the front!"

The heretics were also charging the forward side of our square formation, again emerging from the woods but now with the cavalry leading and the *coseletes* behind. Our harquebusiers again performed their task with the composure of veteran infantry, loading and firing in perfect order with no trace of agitation. Among them I saw Diego Alatriste blow on a slow match, cheek his weapon, and aim. The volley left a large number of Hollanders on the ground, but the main body of soldiers remained, far too many for our own good, and our detachments of harquebusiers, and I with them, were forced to take cover among the pikes. In the confusion I lost sight of my master, and the only one of his comrades I could see was Sebastián Copons—the bandage on his head calling to mind the kerchiefs of his native Aragon—as he put hand to his sword with resolve. A few flustered Spaniards deserted, fleeing past their comrades toward the rear (Iberia did not always give birth to lions), but most stood their ground. Harquebuses blasted, and all around me musket balls dug into flesh. I was showered with a spray of pike man's blood as he fell atop me, invoking the *Madre de Deus* in Portuguese. I slipped from beneath him, freed myself from his lance, which was caught between my legs, only to find myself jostled in the ebb and flow of the battle, immersed in smells of rough, grimy clothing, sweat, powder, and blood.

"Hold! . . . Spain!. . . . Spaaain!"

At our backs, behind the tightly knit rows protecting the standards, the drums beat on relentlessly. More musket balls whirred and more men fell, and each time the rows closed over the gaps they had left, while I stumbled over the armored bodies that lay scattered about me. I could see almost nothing of what was happening in front of me, and I rose to my tiptoes to look over the shoulders of men in buffcoats and leather, steel breastplates and helmets. I was suffocated by the heat and by the smoke of powder. My head was spinning, and with my last shred of lucidity I reached behind me and pulled out my dagger.

"Oñate! . . . Oñate!" I yelled with all my soul.

An instant later, with a crack of pike shafts, screams of wounded horses, and clash of swords, the Dutch Light Horse was upon us, and only God could recognize His own.

6. ATTACK WITHOUT QUARTER

At times I look at the painting, and I remember. Not even
Diego Velázquez, despite everything I told him, was capable of portraying on canvas—it is barely insinuated in the
clouds of smoke and gray fog of the background—the long
and deadly road we had to take to compose such a majestic
scene or the lances that lay along that road and would never
see the sun rise over Breda. I myself was yet to encounter
the blood-dripping steel of those same lances in charnel
houses like Nordlingen and Rocroi, which were, respec-
tively, the dying rays of the Spanish star and a terrible sunset for the army of Flanders. And of those battles, like the
one that morning at the Ruyter mill, I remember especially
the sounds: the cries of the men, the crack of crossed pikes,
the clash of steel against steel, the distinct notes of weapons
ripping clothing, entering flesh, shattering bones. Once,

much later, Angélica de Alquézar asked me in a frivolous tone if there was anything more sinister than the *currrunch* of a hoe cutting into a potato. Without hesitating I replied, "The *cur-rrunch* of steel splitting a skull," and I saw her smile as she stared at me with those blue eyes the devil had granted to her. And then she reached out and with her fingertips touched my eyelids, which were wide open as I again beheld the horror, and then she grazed the mouth that so many times had shouted my fear and my courage and the hands that had gripped steel and spilled blood. She kissed me with her full, warm lips and even smiled as she did it and drew back from me. And now that Angélica is as dead and gone as the Spain I am writing about, I still cannot erase that smile from my memory. It was the same smile that appeared on her lips every time she did something evil, every time she put my life in jeopardy, and every time she kissed my scars, for some of them, *pardiez*, as I have written elsewhere, were caused by her.

I also remember pride. Among the emotions that flash through one's head in combat are, first, fear, then ardor and madness. Later, exhaustion, resignation, and indifference filter into the soldier's soul. But if he survives, and if he is from the good seed from which certain men germinate, there also remains the honor of a duty fulfilled. I am not, Your Mercies, speaking of the soldier's duty to God or to his king, nor of the inept but honorable soldier who fights to collect his pay, not even of the obligation to friends and comrades. I am referring to something else, something I learned at Captain Alatriste's side: the duty to fight when one must, aside from the question of nation and flag, the moral burden of a fight that tends not to be occasioned by either of these but by pure chance. I am speaking of when a man grasps his sword in hand, takes his stance, and demands the true price of his hide rather than simply giving it up like a sheep to the slaughter. I am speaking of recognizing, and seizing, what life rarely offers: an opportunity to lose it with dignity and with honor.

So, I was looking for my master. In the midst of all the fury of sword thrusts, pistol shots, and gutted horses treading on their entrails, I pushed and shoved my way with pounding heart, dagger in hand, yelling for Captain Alatriste. There was death on all sides, but by now no one was killing for his king; they just did not want to give up their lives too cheaply. The first rows of our squad were a pandemonium of Spaniards and Hollanders locked in deadly embrace, their orange or red bands the only guide as to whether one should drive in steel or stand shoulder to shoulder with a comrade.

This was my first experience of real combat, a desperate struggle against everything I identified as the enemy. I had been in my fair share of scrapes: shooting a man in Madrid, crossing steel with Gualterio Malatesta, attacking the gate of Oudkerk, in addition to minor skirmishes here and there in Flanders. Not, if you will forgive me, a trivial record for a youth. And only moments before, my dagger had drawn the last breath from the heretic wounded by Captain Alatriste, whose lifeblood stained my jerkin. But never, never until that Dutch charge, had I been in anything like this, sunk in such madness, to the point where chance counted more than courage or skill. Every man was giving his best in the fight, joining together in a mob of men slipping and sliding over the dead and wounded, stabbing each other on grass slick with blood. Pikes and harquebuses were useless now, even swords were of little use, the best weapon for cutting and slicing and stabbing being a dagger or poniard. I do not know how I managed to stay alive through such havoc, but after a few moments—or was it a century? Even time had stopped running as it should—I found myself, bruised, shaken, filled with a mixture of fright and courage, beside Captain Alatriste and his comrades.

By my faith, but they were wolves. In the chaos of those first rows, my master's squad was grouped together like a formation within a formation, back to back, their swords and daggers so lethal they were like monstrous maws chewing up the enemy. They were not yelling "Spain!" or "Santiago!" to give themselves courage; they fought tight-lipped, saving their breath for killing heretics. God knows they succeeded in this, for there were disemboweled bodies everywhere. Sebastián Copons still had his blood-soaked kerchief around his head; Garrote and Mendieta were wielding broken-off pikes to hold back the Dutch; and Alatriste had his usual dagger in one hand and sword in the other, both of them crimson to the quillons. The Olivares brothers and the Galician Rivas completed the group. As for José Llop, their comrade from Mallorca, he lay on the ground, dead. I was slow to recognize him because a harquebus ball had blown off half his face.

Diego Alatriste seemed to be somewhere far beyond all that. He had thrown off his hat, and tangled, dirty hair fell over his forehead and ears. His legs were planted firmly apart as if nailed to the ground, and all his energy and wrath were concentrated in his eyes, which gleamed red and dangerous in his smoke-blackened face. He fought with calculated efficiency, dealing lethal blows that seemed propelled by hidden springs in his body. He blocked swords and pike blades, slashed out with his dagger, and used each pause in the action to lower his hands and rest a moment before fighting again, as if avariciously conserving the flow of his energy. I worked my way toward him, but he gave no sign of recognition. He was far away, as if he had traveled down a long road and was fighting without looking back, at the very threshold of hell.

My hand was numb from gripping my dagger so tightly, and out of pure clumsiness I dropped it. I bent down to pick it up, and when I stood, I saw Hollanders rushing toward us, shouting at the top of their lungs: Musket balls were whizzing by, and a wall of pikes crashed above my head. I sensed men dropping around me, and again I gripped my dagger, wanting nothing more than to be out of the fray, convinced that my hour had come. Something struck a blow to my head that staggered me, and countless pinpoints of light swam before my eyes. I half-fainted, but I did not let go of my dagger, determined to carry it with me to wherever I was going. All I wanted was not to be found without it in my hand. Then I thought of my mother, and I prayed. *Padre Nuestro*—Our Father—suddenly flashed into my mind. *"Gure Aita, Padre nuestro,"* I repeated over and over in Basque and in Spanish, dazed, unable to remember the rest of the prayer. In that instant someone grabbed my jerkin and dragged me across the grass, over the dead and wounded. Blindly, I made two weak swings with my blade, thinking I was dealing with an enemy, until I felt a pinch on the nape of my neck and then another that stopped my pitiful swipes. I was deposited inside a small circle of legs and mud-stained boots, overhearing the clash of weapons—*clinnng, cur-rac, swish-swash, cloc, chasss*—a sinister concert of torn flesh, shattered bones, and guttural sounds from throats exhaling fury, pain, fear, and agony. In the background, behind the rows still holding firm around our standards, the proud, impassive, *tum-tum-tum* of the drum continued to beat for our poor old Spain.

"They're falling back! . . . After them! . . . They're falling back!"

The *tercio* had held. So many men in the first rows lay where they had fallen that the piles of corpses replicated the formation as it had been at the beginning of the battle. Bugles were blowing, and the sound of the drum was more intense as more were now headed our way. Along the dike and the Ruyter mill road we saw fluttering banners and relief pikes coming to our aid. A squad of Italian cavalry carrying harquebusiers on the croups of their mounts galloped past our flank, the horsemen saluting as they raced by to overrun the Dutch, who had come for wool and instead been shorn themselves and were retreating in defeat and gratifying disorder, seeking the safety of the woods. The vanguard of our comrades, *coseletes, pike men, with short lances and musketeers, had already reached the field on the other side of the road, where Soest's Walloon* tercio *had been chopped to pieces, albeit with no little honor.*

"After them! After them! . . . Close in for Spain! . . . Close in!"

Our camp was yelling victory at the top of their voices, and men who had fought all morning in obstinate silence were exuberantly calling out the names of the *Virgen Santísima* and Santiago. Exhausted veterans set down their weapons to kiss rosaries and medallions. The drum was pounding without mercy, without quarter, marking the pursuit and capture of the conquered enemy, a time for collecting spoils and for making them pay dearly for our dead and for the arduous day they had put us through. The lines of the *tercio* were breaking up to chase after the heretics, catching first the wounded and the stragglers, then splitting open heads, lopping off limbs, and cutting throats. In short, mercy for no man. For if the Spanish infantry was fierce in attacking or defending, it was twice as fierce when taking revenge. The Italians and Walloons were not far behind, the latter fervently desiring blood in return for that which their Soest comrades had shed. The landscape was dotted with thousands of men racing about helter-skelter, killing, then killing again, pillaging the wounded and dead scattered across the field, so badly butchered that at times the most intact body piece was an ear.

Captain Alatriste and his comrades were participating like everyone else, as heatedly as Your Mercies could imagine. I was trying to keep up with them, still stunned by the melee and by the egg-sized lump on my head but yelling as wildly as any. Along the way, I took a splendid short Solingen sword from the first dead enemy I came across and, sheathing my dagger, moved on, thrusting that fine German blade at anything dead or alive in my path, like someone stabbing blood sausages. It was carnage, game, and madness all rolled into one, and what had once been a battle had turned into a slaughter of young English bulls and Flemish cuts. Some did not even defend themselves, like the group we caught up with splashing waist deep in a peat bog. There, we descended on them, taking a fine catch of Calvinists, plunging our swords into them, slicing and ripping right and left, deaf to their pleas and to up-raised hands begging for mercy, until the blackish water was bright red and they were floating in it like chopped tuna fish.

We did a lot of killing, for we had a place to do it. And since there were so many, we could not stop with a few. The hunt went on for a league and lasted till nightfall, and by then my fellow *mochileros* had joined in, along with local peasants who knew no band other than their greed, and even some vivandières, whores, and sutlers who had mi-grated to Oudkerk, drawn by the smell of booty. They fol-lowed after the soldiers, plundering anything that was left, a flock of crows leaving in their passing nothing but naked corpses. I was still in the chase, keeping up with those in the vanguard, not feeling the exhaustion of the day, as if fury and desire for revenge had given me strength to go on to the end of the world. I was—and may God forgive me if it be His wish—hoarse from yelling and red with the blood of those wretched Dutch. A pink dusk was closing over the burning villages on the far side of the forest, and there was no canal, no path, no road along the dike that was free of the dead. At that point, bone-weary, we stopped by a small cluster of five or six houses where even the domestic animals had been killed. A group of Dutch stragglers had hidden there, and finishing them off took the last moments of light. Finally, in the reddish glow of burning roofs, we calmed down, little by little, our pouches stuffed with booty, and here and there men began to drop to the ground, suddenly seized by untold fatigue, breathing like beaten animals. Only a fool maintains that victory is joy. As our senses slowly returned we fell silent, avoiding one another's eyes, as if ashamed of our filthy hair standing on end, our black, strained faces, reddened eyes, the crust of blood drying on our clothing and weapons. Now the only sound was the sputtering of the fire and creaking of beams collapsing among the flames, but occasionally from the night around us came shouts and gunfire from those who continued the kill.

Bruised and battered, I squatted down by the side of a house, my back against the wall. My eyes were tearing; I was breathing with difficulty and was tortured by thirst. In the light of the fire I saw Curro Garrote knotting into a cloth the rings, chains, and silver buttons he had scavenged from the dead. Mendieta was stretched out face down; you would have thought he was as stone-cold dead as the Hollander corpses strewn about were it not for his raucous snores. Other Spaniards were sitting in groups or alone, and among them I thought I recognized Captain Bragado with one arm in a sling. Gradually low-pitched voices reached my ears, mostly queries about the fate of some comrade or other. Someone asked about Llop and was answered by silence. A few men made small fires to roast strips of meat they had cut from the dead farm animals, and soldiers slowly began to congregate around the flames. After a while they were talking in normal voices, and then someone said something, a comment or a jest, that drew a laugh. I remember the profound impression that laugh made on me, for I had come to believe that at the end of that long day men's laughter had vanished forever from the face of the earth.

I turned toward Captain Alatriste and saw that he was looking at me. He was sitting against the wall a few paces away, with his legs drawn up and his arms around his knees. He was still holding his harquebus. Sebastián

Copons was by his side, his head resting against the wall, his sword between his legs. His face was marred by the large dark scab on his temple that had been revealed when his bandage slipped down around his neck. The men's outlines were etched against the glow from a house burning nearby, brighter from time to time as the flames leaped and played. Diego Alatriste's eyes, gleaming in the firelight, were observing me with a kind of quizzical intensity, as if he were trying to read inside me. I was both ashamed and proud, exhausted yet with an energy that made my heart pound, horrified, sad, bitter, but happy to be alive. And I swear to Your Mercies that following a battle, a man can harbor all these sensations and emotions, and many more, at the same time. The captain kept watching me in silence, more a scrutiny than anything else, to the point that finally I began to feel uncomfortable. I had expected praise, an encouraging smile, something that expressed his esteem for my having conducted myself like a man. That was why I was disconcerted by that observation in which I could discern nothing other than the imperturbable absorption I had seen on other occasions: an expression, or absence of expression, that I could never penetrate. Nor could I until many years later when one day, now a full-grown man, I was surprised to find that I too had, or thought I had, that same gaze.

Uncomfortable, I decided to do something to break the

tension. I stretched my aching body, put the German sword in my belt beside the dagger, and got to my feet.

"Shall I look for something to eat and drink, Captain?"

Light from the flames danced on his face. It was several moments before he answered, and when he did he limited himself to a nod, his aquiline face long beneath the thick mustache. He never took his eyes from me as I turned and followed my shadow.

The conflagration outside cast its light though an open window, tingeing the walls with red. Everywhere the house was in chaos: broken furniture, scorched curtains on the floor, drawers upside down, scattered belongings. Rubble crunched beneath my feet as I walked back and forth looking for a cupboard or some larder not yet ransacked by our rapacious comrades. I remember the immense sadness that permeated that dark, plundered dwelling, the lives that had given warmth to its rooms now gone, the desolation and ruin of what once had been a hearth where undoubtedly a child had laughed and two adults had exchanged tender caresses and words of love. And so the curiosity of someone prowling at will through a place to which he would ordinarily not be invited gave way to a growing melancholy. I thought of my own home in Oñate caught in the destruction of war, of my poor mother and little sisters fleeing, or perhaps worse, their rooms trampled through by some young foreigner who, like me, saw spread across the floor the broken, burned, humble remains of our memories and our lives. And with the selfishness natural in a soldier, I was happy to be in Flanders and not in Spain. I can assure Your Mercies that in the business of war, the misfortunes visited on foreigners are always of some consolation. And at such times, the person who has no one in the world and who risks no fondness for anything but his own skin, is to be envied.

I found nothing worth the search. I stopped a moment to relieve myself against the wall and was buttoning my trousers when something stopped me short. I held my breath an instant, listening, and then I heard it again. It was a prolonged moan, a weak lament coming from the far end of a narrow corridor filled with debris. I might have thought it was an animal in pain except that from time to time I could hear a human timbre. So, quietly, I unsheathed my dagger—in such a narrow space my newly acquired sword was not manageable—and, back to the wall, I slipped closer to find out what it was.

There was enough light from the fires outside to light half the room, projecting shadows with reddish outlines onto a wall covered with a slashed tapestry. Beneath that hanging, propped in the niche between the wall and a battered armoire, slumped a man. The light glinting from his breastplate confirmed that he was a soldier and illuminated a long, blond, tangled head of hair filthy with mud and blood, very pale eyes, and a terrible burn that had left one whole side of his face raw. He was motionless, his eyes staring into the light coming through the window, and from his half-opened lips issued the lament I had heard from the corridor: a hushed, constant moaning interrupted at times by incomprehensible words spoken in a strange tongue.

I crept toward him, cautious, still holding the dagger and watching his hands to ascertain whether he was holding a weapon, though that poor wretch was not in any condition to hold a thing. He looked like a traveler sitting by the shore of the Styx, someone the boatman Charon had left behind, forgotten, on his last crossing. I crouched down beside him, examining him with curiosity; he seemed not to be aware I was there. He kept staring toward the window, motionless, uttering that interminable keening, those fragmented, unrecognizable words, even when I touched his arm with the tip of my dagger. His face was a frightening representation of Janus: one side reasonably intact, the other a pudding of raw flesh glittering with droplets of blood. His hands, too, had been burned. I had seen several dead Hollanders in the flaming stables at the back of the house, and I surmised that this man, wounded in the skirmish, had dragged himself through the smoldering embers to take refuge here.

"*Flamink?*" I asked.

There was no answer but his endless groans. I concluded that he was a young man, not much older than I, and by the breastplate and clothing, was one of the soldiers from the Light Horse that had charged us that morning near the Ruyter mill. Perhaps we had fought near each other when the Dutch and English attempted to break through our formation and we Spaniards desperately fought for our lives. War, I reasoned, took strange twists and turns, curious swings of fortune. Nevertheless, with the horror of the day behind me and the Dutch on the run, I felt neither hostility nor rancor. I had seen many Spaniards die that day but even more enemies. At the moment, the scales were balanced; this was a defenseless man, and I was sated with blood, so I put away my dagger and went outside to Captain Alatriste and the others.

"There is a man inside," I said. "A soldier."

The captain, who had not changed position since I left, scarcely bothered to look up.

"Spanish or Dutch?"

"Dutch, I think. Or English. And he's wounded."

Alatriste nodded slowly, as if at this hour of the night it would have been strange to come across a heretic alive and in good health. Then he shrugged his shoulders, as if asking me why I had come to tell him this.

"I thought," I suggested, "that we might help him."

At last he looked at me, and he did so very slowly; in the firelight I watched his head turn toward me.

"You thought," he murmured.

"Yes."

For another moment he said nothing, just stared at me. Then he half-turned toward Sebastián Copons, still by his side, head against the wall, mouth closed, the bloody kerchief loose around his neck. Alatriste exchanged a glance with him and then looked back toward me. In the long silence I heard the flames crackling.

"You thought," he repeated, absorbed.

Painfully he got to his feet, as if he were numb all over and it cost him to his very bones even to move an inch. He seemed reluctant and very weary. I watched Copons get up and join him.

"Where is he?"

"In the house."

I led them through the rooms and down the corridor to the back. The heretic was still propped between the armoire and the wall. Alatriste stopped on the threshold and looked around before going over to him. He bent down a little and observed him.

"He is Dutch," he concluded finally.

"Can we help him?" I asked.

Captain Alatriste's shadow on the wall did not move.

"Of course."

I felt Sebastián Copons pass by me. His boots shuffled through the broken crockery on the floor as he approached the wounded man. Then Alatriste came over to me and Copons reached toward the sheath over his kidneys and pulled out his *vizcaína*.

"Let's go," the captain said.

Stupefied, I resisted the pressure of his hand on my shoulder, as I watched Copons place his dagger to the neck of the Dutch soldier and slit his throat from ear to ear. Shaking, I raised my eyes toward Alatriste's dark face. I could not see his eyes, though I knew they were on me.

"H-h-he was . . . ," I stammered.

Then I stopped, for words suddenly seemed pointless. With an involuntary gesture of rejection, I shook the captain's hand from my shoulder, but he kept it there, holding on like an iron clamp. Copons stood up, and after cleaning the blade of his dagger on the victim's clothing, replaced it in its sheath. Then he went out into the corridor before I could even blink.

I turned brusquely, feeling my shoulder at last free. I took two steps toward the young man who was now dead. Nothing about the scene had changed, except that his lament had ceased and a dark, thick, shining veil had descended from the gorget of his armor, the red blending with the splendor of the firelight at the window. He seemed more alone than before; a solitude so pitiable that I felt an intense, deep pain, as if it were I, or part of me, who was sitting on that floor, back against the wall, eyes fixed and open, staring at the night. I know, I thought, that someone somewhere is waiting for the return of this man who won't be going anywhere. Perhaps a mother, a sweetheart, a sister, or a father is praying for him, for his health, for his life, for his return. And there may be a bed where he slept as a boy and a landscape he watched grow and change. And no one there knows he is dead.

I do not know how long I stood there, silently staring at the corpse, but after a while I heard a stirring, and without having to turn I knew that Captain Alatriste had stayed there all the time by my side. I smelled the familiar harsh scent of sweat, leather, and the metal of his clothing and weapons, and then I heard his voice.

"A man knows when the end has come. That man knew."

I did not answer. I was still contemplating the corpse's slit throat. Now his blood was forming an enormous dark stain around his legs, which were stretched out in front of him. It is incredible, I thought, the amount of blood we have in our bodies, at least two or three *azumbres*, and how easy it is to spill it.

"That is all we could do for him," Alatriste added.

Again I had no answer and stood a while longer without speaking. Finally I heard him move again. Alatriste came close a moment, as if wondering whether or not to speak to me, as if there were countless unspoken words between us that would never be said if he did not say them now. But he said nothing, and finally his footsteps headed toward the corridor.

It was then that I turned around. I felt a mute, tranquil rage that I had never known until that night. A desperate anger, as bitter as Alatriste's own silences.

"Do you mean to say, Your Mercy, Captain, that we have just performed a good work? A good service?"

I had never spoken to him in that tone before. The footsteps stopped, and Alatriste's voice sounded strangely opaque. I imagined his gray-green eyes in the penumbra, staring vacantly into the void.

"When the moment comes," he said, "pray to God that someone will do the same for you."

That is what happened that night when Sebastián Copons slit the throat of the wounded Hollander and I shrugged away Captain Alatriste's hand. That was how, scarcely without realizing, I crossed that shadowy line that every lucid man crosses sooner or later. There, alone, standing before that corpse, I began to look at the world in a very different way. I knew myself in possession of a terrible truth that until that instant I had intuited only in Captain Alatriste's glaucous gaze: He who kills from afar knows nothing at all about the act of killing. He who kills from afar derives no lesson from life or from death; he neither risks nor stains his hands with blood, nor hears the breathing of his adversary, nor reads the fear, courage, or indifference in his eyes. He who kills from afar tests neither his arm, his heart, or his conscience, nor does he create ghosts that will later haunt him every single night for the rest of his life. He who kills from afar is a knave who commends to others the dirty and terrible task that is his own. He who kills from afar is worse than other men, because he does not know anger, loathing, and vengeance, the terrible passion of flesh and of blood as they meet steel, but he is equally innocent of pity and remorse. For that reason, he who kills from afar does not know what he has lost.

7. THE SIEGE

*From Íñigo Balboa to don Francisco de Quevedo
Villegas * To his attention in the Tavern of the Turk
* On Calle de Toledo near La Puerta
Cerrada, Madrid.*

Esteemed don Francisco:

*I am writing to Your Mercy at the request of
Captain Alatriste so that you may see, he says, the
progress I am making with the written word. Please,
however, excuse the errors. I can tell you that I am
continuing with my reading, when that is possible,
and seizing the opportunity to practice good
penmanship whenever I can. In idle moments, which
in the life of a* mochilero *and that of a soldier are
as many or more than others have, I am learning*

from Padre Salanueva the declinations and verbs in
Latin. Padre Salanueva is chaplain of our tercio,
and as the soldiers say, he is many leagues from
being a man of God, but he owes money or favors to
my master. The fact is that he treats me with
fondness and devotes the time he is sober (he is one
of those who drinks more wine than he consecrates)
to bettering my education with Caesar's
Commentaries *and such religious books as the Old*
and New Testaments. And speaking of books, I must
thank you, Your Mercy, for sending me El
ingenioso caballero don Quijote de la Mancha,
second part of El ingenioso hidalgo, *which I am*
reading with the same pleasure and diligence as
the first.

As to our life in Flanders, you will, Y.M., know
that it has undergone some changes in recent times.
With winter's end, our duty along the Ooster canal
ended as well. The old Cartagena tercio *is now to*
be found beneath the very walls of Breda, taking
part in a siege. It is a hard life, for the Dutch have
fortified their stronghold well, and everything is
sap and countersap, mine and countermine, trench
and tunnel, so that our travails are more similar to
a mole's than a soldier's. This life is nothing but
discomfort, dirt, and lice beyond endurance and,

furthermore, a labor exposed to attacks made from the stronghold and constant fire from their harquebusiers. The walls of the town are not of brick but of dirt. That makes it difficult to dig out a sap, or tunnel, because of the assault of our artillery battery. The walls are supported by fifteen well-protected bulwarks and surrounded by fosses—water-filled ditches—with fourteen ravelins, all of it so well arranged that each of the walls, bulwarks, ravelins, and fosses works in defense of the other, so much so that our approaches have been extremely difficult, costing labor and lives.

The defense of the city is in the hands of Justin of Nassau, a Dutchman and a relative of the other Nassau, Maurice. And consider that at the Ginneken gate he has French and Walloons, English at the Den Bosch gate, and Flemish and Scots at the Antwerp gate, all of them conversant in matters of war, so that it is not possible to take the town by assault. Thence the necessity for the patient encirclement, which our general don Ambrosio Spínola is maintaining with great effort and sacrifice, using fifteen tercios *from Catholic nations. Among them are Spaniards, as would be expected, the least in number but it is they who are always*

*called on for dangerous tasks that require
experienced and disciplined men.*

*You would marvel, Y.M., if you saw with your
own eyes the ingenuity of the siege tactics and the
inventiveness with which they have been conceived.
They are the amazement of the whole of Europe,
for each village and fort around the town are united
by trenches and bulwarks to impede the sorties of
the besieged and to prevent them from receiving aid
from outside. In our camp, weeks at a time go by
when we use the pick and the trenching spade more
often than the pike and the harquebus.*

*This country is flat, with meadows and trees,
little wine, and insalubrious water, and it is now
devastated and destitute from the war, so that
provisions are becoming scarce indeed. A measure
of wheat—when it can be found—costs eight florins.
Even the price of turnip seeds is up in the clouds.
The villagers and suppliers from nearby towns dare
not, unless by stealth, bring anything to our camp.
Some Spanish soldiers, who care less for their
reputation than for their hunger, eat the meat of
dead horses, which is wretched provender. We
mochileros go out to forage, sometimes traveling
far, even in enemy territory, where we risk exposure
to the heretic cavalry that at times overtakes our*

scattered scavengers and kills us at will. I myself
have found myself entrusting my health no few
times to the fleetness of my legs. Want is
widespread, as I said, as much in our trenches as
within the city. That plays to our benefit, and to that
of the true religion, for the French, English, Scots,
and Flemish garrisoned in the town, accustomed to
a life of greater indulgence, suffer more from
hunger and privations than those of our camp and
especially we Spaniards. For our camp is mostly old
soldiers used to suffering inside Spain and to
fighting outside of it, with no need for succor other
than a crust of hard bread and a little water or wine
to continue the fight.

And as to our own health, I am doing well.
Tomorrow will mark my fifteenth birthday, and I
have grown several inches. Captain Alatriste is as
he always is, with little meat on his bones and few
words in his mouth. These privations seem not to
affect him unduly. Perhaps because, as he says
(twisting his mustache with one of those grimaces
that could be taken as a smile), he has done without
for most of his life, and the soldier becomes
accustomed to everything, especially misery. You
are already aware that he is a man little given to
taking up a quill to write a letter. But he charges me

*to tell you that he appreciates yours. He also bids
me greet you with all his deference and all his
affection. And asks that you convey the same to his
friends at the Tavern of the Turk, and to
La Lebrijana.*

*And one last thing. I know from the captain
that Y.M. is often in the palace these days. That
being the case, it is possible that you may come
across a girl, or young lady, named Angélica de
Alquézar, whose acquaintance you must already
have made. She was, and perhaps is still, a menina
serving her majesty the queen. Should you in fact
meet her, I would ask of you a very particular
service. If the occasion arises, will you tell her that
Íñigo Balboa is in Flanders serving our lord and
king and the holy Catholic faith, and that he has
learned to fight honorably, like a Spaniard and a
soldier? Should you do this for me, my most
esteemed don Francisco, the affection and
friendship I have always professed for you will be
greater still.*

May God care for you and care for us all.
Íñigo Balboa Aguirre
*(Written beneath the walls of Breda, the first
day of April of one thousand six hundred twenty-
five)*

From the trench I could hear the Hollanders digging. Diego Alatriste clamped his ear to one of the piles driven into the ground to support the fascines and gabions of the sap, and once again heard the muffled *rrish-rrish* traveling through the entrails of the earth. For a week now the soldiers in Breda had been working night and day to intercept the trench and mine we were digging toward the ravelin they called The Cemetery. Inch by inch, our men were advancing with our mine and the enemy with their countermine; we planning to set barrels of powder to explode beneath the Dutch fortifications and they determined to set off a friendly blast beneath the feet of the Catholic king's sappers. It was all a question of hard work and speed, of who dug more quickly and was able to light his fuses first.

"Accursed animal," said Garrote.

His head was cocked and his eyes alert, a typical stance, positioned behind the gabions with his musket pointed between boards serving as an embrasure, its cord soaked and smoking. He wrinkled his nose, nauseated. The "accursed animal" was a mule that had been lying dead in the sun for three days only a short distance from the trench on land claimed by neither side. It had strayed from the Spanish camp and had had time to sashay back and forth between enemy positions until a musket ball fired from the wall, *zap!*, stopped it in its tracks, and now it lay there, feet in the air, stinking, and buzzing with flies.

"You've been there a long time, and you haven't got a Hollander yet," Mendieta commented.

"I almost have," said Garrote.

Mendieta was sitting at the bottom of the sap, at Garrote's feet, picking off lice with solemn Basque meticulousness: In the trenches, not content with living like kings in our hair and our rags, lice would come out and stroll around like Madrid gentlemen. The Biscayan had spoken without much interest, absorbed in his task. His beard was untrimmed and his clothing torn and grimy, like everyone else's there, including Alatriste himself.

"Can you see him, more or less?"

Garrote nodded. He had taken off his hat to offer less of a target for the harquebusiers across the way. His curly hair was caught back in a greasy ponytail.

"Not now, no. But once in a while he chances a look, and the next time I'll have the whoreson."

Alatriste ventured a quick look of his own above the parapet, attempting to stay under the cover of the timber and fascines. The man was perhaps one of the Dutch sappers working at the mouth of their tunnel some twenty *varas* ahead, well within range. However much he tried to remain hidden, his digging exposed him a little, not too much, barely his head, but enough for Garrote, who was not in any hurry and was considered a fine marksman, to keep him in sight until he had a sure shot. The Malagueño, a man who believed in give and take, wanted to return the favor of the mule.

Some eighteen or twenty Spaniards were in the trench, one of the most advanced, which zigzagged along a short distance away from the Dutch positions. Diego Alatriste's squad spent two weeks of every three there, with the rest of Captain Bragado's *bandera*, distributed among the nearby saps and fosses, all of them situated between The Cemetery ravelin and the Merck River, at two lengths of a harquebus shot from the main wall and citadel of Breda.

"Ah, here's my heretic," Garrote murmured.

Mendieta, who had just found a louse and was examining it with familiar curiosity before crushing it between his fingernails, looked up with interest.

"You have a Hollander?"

"I have him."

"Speed him to hell, then."

"That is my plan."

After running his tongue over his lips, Garrote had blown on the cord of his harquebus and was now carefully cheeking the musket, half-closing his left eye, his index finger caressing the trigger as if it were the nipple of a half-ducat harlot. Rising up a little farther, Alatriste had a fleeting view of an incautious bare head sticking up from the Dutch trench.

"Another maggot dying in mortal sin," he heard Garrote comment.

Then came the sound of the shot, and with the flash of scorched powder Alatriste saw the head disappear. Three or four yells of fury followed, and three or four musket balls threw up earth on the Spanish parapet. Garrote, who had sunk back down again into the trench, laughed to himself, his smoking musket propped between his legs. Outside he heard more shots and insults shouted in Flemish.

"Tell them to go bugger themselves," said Mendieta, locating another louse.

Sebastián Copons opened one eye and closed it again. Garrote's musket fire had interrupted his siesta at the foot of the parapet, his head resting on a filthy blanket. The Olivares brothers, curious, poked their bushy heads around a corner of the trench. Alatriste had crouched down and was sitting with his back against the terreplein. He dug through his pouch, searching for the chunk of hard black bread he had put there the day before. He put it in his mouth and moistened it with saliva before he began chewing it, ever so slowly. With the stench of the dead mule and the foul air in the sap it was not an exquisite repast, but neither was there much choice, and even a simple crust of bread was a feast worthy of a king. No one would bring new provisions until nightfall, under the shelter of darkness.

Medieta allowed the new louse to crawl down the back of his hand. Finally, bored with the game, he crushed it. Garrote was cleaning the still-warm barrel of his harquebus with a ramrod, humming an Italian tune.

"Oh, to be in Naples," he said after a bit, flashing a smile that gleamed white in his swarthy Moorish face.

Everyone knew that Curro Garrote had served two years in the *tercio* of Sicily and four in Naples, forced to make a change of scene following a number of murky adventures involving women, knives, nocturnal burglaries, and a death, obligatory time spent in the prison of Vicaría, and another, voluntary, stay in the safe haven of the church of La Capela, a well-known bolt-hole.

To he who left me his cape,
and fleeing from me, escaped,
what can the Law hope?
when in the land of the Pope
he'll not pay his part in the scrape.

So between one thing and another, Garrote had sailed with the galleys of our lord and king along the Barbary Coast and in the Aegean Sea, plundering the land of the infidels and pirating carmoussels and other Turkish vessels. During those years, he said, he had collected sufficient booty to retire without any worries. And so he would have done had he not crossed paths with too many women and been so irresistibly drawn to gaming. For at the sight of a pair of dice or deck of cards, the Malagueño was one of those men who play hard and are capable of gambling away the sun before it comes up.

"Italy," he repeated in a low voice, with a faraway look and a rascally smile lingering on his lips.

He said it the way one pronounces the name of a woman, and Captain Alatriste could understand why. Although he did not speak freely as Garrote did, he, too, had his recollections of Italy, which must have seemed even more pleasant in a trench in Flanders. Like every soldier who had been posted there, he longed for that land; or perhaps what he truly longed for was to be young again beneath the generous blue skies of the Mediterranean. At twenty-seven, after being mustered out of his *tercio* following the suppression of rebellious Moors in Valencia, he had enlisted in the *tercio* of Naples and fought against Turks, Berbers, and Venetians. On the galleys of the Marqués de Santa Cruz his eyes had seen the infidel squadrons blaze before La Goleta; with Captain Contreras, the isles of the Adriatic; and in the fateful shallows of the Kerkennahs, he had witnessed the water turn red with Spanish blood. Aided by a companion named Diego Duque de Estrada, he escaped from that place dragging the young and badly wounded Álvaro de la Marca, the future Conde de Guadalmedina.

During those years of his youth, good fortune and the delights of Italy had alternated with no few labors and perils, although none could embitter the sweet recollection of the arbors of grapes on the gentle slopes of Vesuvius, the comrades, the music, the wine in the Chorrillo tavern, and the beautiful women. Between good and bad times, in the year '13, his galley was captured at the mouth of the Constantinople canal, riddled to the mast top with Turks' arrows and with half its crew cut to ribbons. Wounded in one leg, Alatriste was liberated when the ship holding him captive was captured in turn. Two years later, the fifteenth of the century, when Alatriste had reached the age of Christ, he was one of sixteen hundred Spaniards and Italians who, with a flotilla of five ships, despoiled the coast of the Levant for four months, later disembarking in Naples with a wealth of booty. There, once again, the wheel of Fortune spun, and his life was turned upside down. An olive-skinned woman, half Italian and half Spanish, with dark hair and large eyes—the kind who claims to be frightened when she sees a mouse but is perfectly relaxed with half a company of harquebusiers— had begun by asking him for a gift of some Genoa plums, then it was a gold necklace, and finally silk gowns. It ended, as often happens, when she had purged him of his last *maravedí*. Then the plot thickened, in the style of Lope's plays, with an inopportune visit and a stranger in a nightshirt in a place he shouldn't be. The sight of the alternate in his shirttails substantially weakened the credence of the little minx's protests as, wide-eyed, she identified the fellow as her cousin, though he seemed to be more what the English would call a kissing cousin. Furthermore, Diego Alatriste was far too old to have the wool pulled over his eyes so easily. So, after one of the woman's cheeks had been embellished by an oblique cut with the knife, and the intruder in the nightshirt by half a sword blade through his chest—in his haste this presumed cousin had come out to fight without his breeches, which seemed to have diminished his brio at the hour when it came to proving himself a good swordsman—Diego Alatriste took to his heels before being hauled off to prison. A precaution which, at that juncture, consisted of a hasty departure for Spain, thanks to the favor granted by an old acquaintance, the previously mentioned Alonso de Contreras, with whom, both only lads, he had left for Flanders at the age of thirteen, following the standards of Prince Albert.

"Here comes Bragado," said Garrote.

Captain Carmelo Bragado was coming along the trench, head lowered and hat in hand to offer less of a target, searching out the defilade of enemy harquebusiers posted on the ravelin. Even so, as this robust man from León's strapping six feet were difficult to hide from Dutch eyes, a pair of musket shots came, *ziiing, zaaang*, whirring over the parapet in homage to his arrival.

"May God visit them with the pox," growled Bragado, dropping down between Copons and Alatriste.

He was fanning his sweaty face with the hat in his right hand and resting the left on the hilt of his Toledo blade; that hand, injured in the combat at the Ruyter mill, was missing the first two joints of the ring and little fingers. After a while, just as Diego Alatriste had done before him, he put an ear to one of the posts in the ground and frowned.

"Those heretic moles are in a hurry," he said.

He leaned back, scratching his mustache where sweat had dripped onto it from the tip of his nose.

"I bring two items of bad news," he added after a while.

He regarded the misery of the trenches, the debris piled everywhere, the deplorable appearance of the soldiers. His nose wrinkled at the stench from the dead mule.

"Although, among Spaniards," he quipped, "having only two items of bad news is always good news."

More time passed before he spoke again; finally he grimaced and again scratched his nose.

"They killed Ulloa last night."

Someone muttered, "S'blood!" but the others said nothing. Ulloa was a squad corporal, an old soldier with whom they had shared good camaraderie until he earned his final bonus. As Bragado reported in few words, he had gone out to reconnoiter the Dutch trenches with an Italian sergeant, and only the Italian returned.

"With whom did he leave a testament?" Garrote asked with interest.

"With me," Bragado replied. "A third goes to paying for masses."

For a time they were silent, and that was all the epitaph Ulloa would receive. Copons went back to his siesta and Mendieta to his quest for lice. Garrote, who had finished cleaning his musket, was chewing his nails and spitting out pieces as black as his soul.

"How is our mine going?" Alatriste wanted to know.

Bragado gave a shrug.

"Very slow. The sappers have run into mud that's too soft, and water is seeping in from the river. They have a lot of shoring up to do, and that takes time. We fear that the heretics will get to us first and relieve us of our bollocks."

They heard shots at the far end of the trench, out of view; a heavy volley that lasted only an instant, then everything was calm again. Alatriste looked at his captain, waiting for him to get to impart the other bad news. Bragado never visited them just for the pleasure of stretching his legs.

"Gentlemen," he said finally, "you have been assigned to the caponnieres."

"God's bones!" Garrote blasphemed.

The caponnieres were narrow tunnels excavated by sappers who, protected overhead by blankets, wood, and gabion baskets, dug below the trenches. These burrows were used both for aborting the advance of enemy works and for tunneling deeper in order to reach fosses, saps, and ditches where the men could then explode petards and smoke out the adversary with sulfur and wet straw. It was a grisly way to fight: below ground, in the dark, in passageways so narrow that often the men could move only by crawling along, one by one, choked by heat, dust, and sulfur fumes, engaging opponents like blind moles. The caponnieres near The Cemetery ravelin twisted and turned around the Spaniards' main tunnel and were very close to those of the Dutch, attempting to counter the enemies' efforts with their own; often when the soldiers collapsed a wall with a pick or a petard, they came face to face with the sappers on the other side in a melee of flashing daggers and point-blank pistol shots and, of course, the short-handled spades that, for this very reason, were sharpened with whetstones until the edges were keen as knives.

"It is time," said Diego Alatriste.

He was crouched at the entrance of the main tunnel with his band, and Captain Bragado was watching from a short distance away in the sap, kneeling with the rest of

Alatriste's squad and a dozen more from his *bandera*, ready to lend a hand if the occasion demanded. Alatriste was accompanied by Mendieta, Copons, Garrote, the Galician Rivas, and the two Olivares brothers. Manuel Rivas was an extremely trustworthy and courageous youth, a fine boned, blue-eyed lad who spoke a less-than-exemplary Spanish with the strong accent of Finisterre. As for the Olivares, they looked like twins, though they weren't. They had very similar features, with Gypsy-like faces and hair, and thick black beards edging up to generous Semitic noses that from a league away shouted the presence of great-grandparents who would have balked at eating bacon. That mattered not one whit to their comrades, for questions of purity of blood never arose in the *tercios;* it was believed that if a man spilled his blood in battle, that blood had circulated through pure hidalgo veins. The two brothers were always together: They slept back to back, shared every last crumb of bread, and watched out for each other in battle.

"Who will go first?" asked Alatriste.

Garrote did not step forward, apparently absorbed in running his finger along the edge of his dagger blade. Pale, and with a grimace, Rivas made as if to move forward, but Copons, economical as usual in both actions and words, picked up some straws from the ground and offered them to his comrades. It was Mendieta who drew the shortest. He looked at it for a long time and then without a word adjusted his dagger, laid his hat and sword on the ground, picked up the small primed pistol Alatriste handed him, and entered the tunnel, carrying a short, very sharp spade in the other hand. Behind him went Alatriste and Copons, they too removing hats and swords and tightening their leather buffcoats. The others followed in single file as Bragado and those staying behind watched in silence.

The beginning of the main gallery was lit by a pitch torch, its oily light illuminating the sweat on the naked torsos of the German sappers who had taken a break in their labors and were leaning on their picks and spades as they watched the men pass. The Germans were as good at digging as they were at fighting, especially when they were sober and well paid. Even their women, who, laden like mules, were coming and going with provisions from the camp, did their part by carrying large baskets and tools. Their corporal, a red-bearded fellow with arms like Alpujarras hams, guided the group through the labyrinth of passages. The tunnel grew lower and narrower the closer they came to the Dutch lines. Finally the sapper stopped at the mouth of a caponniere no more than three feet high. Light from a hanging oil lamp fell on a slow fuse that disappeared into the darkness, sinister as a black serpent.

"*Eine vara*, one," said the German, indicating with spread hands the width of the earthen wall that separated the end of the caponniere from the Dutch passageway.

Alatriste nodded, and they all moved away from the opening, backs against the wall as they knotted kerchiefs around their faces to protect mouths and noses. The German gave them a big smile.

"Zum Teufel!" he said. Then he picked up the lantern and lit the fuse.

Bones. The tunnel ran beneath the cemetery, and now bones were dropping down everywhere, mixed with earth. Long bones and short, fleshless skulls, tibias, vertebrae. Whole skeletons shrouded in torn and dirty winding sheets, clothing reduced to shreds by time. These remnants were mixed with dust and rubble, rotted splinters of coffins, fragments of headstones, and a nauseating stench flooded the caponniere. After the explosion, Diego Alatriste and the other men started to crawl toward the breach, crossing paths with rats squealing in terror. There was an opening to the sky that allowed a little light and air to filter through, and they passed beneath that pale glimmer, veiled in the smoke of burnt powder, before entering the shadows on the other side, the source of moans and cries in foreign voices. Alatriste was wet with sweat beneath his buffcoat, and his mouth was dry and gritty behind the protective kerchief. He dragged himself forward on his elbows. Something round rolled toward him, pushed by the feet of the man ahead of him; it was a human skull. The rest of a skeleton shattered from its coffin by the explosion and the subsequent collapse shifted beneath his arms as he pulled himself over the remains and splintered bones scraped his thighs.

He was not thinking. He crawled along inch by inch, jaws clenched and eyes closed to keep out the dirt, barely able to breathe. He felt nothing. Muscles knotted with tension were indifferent to any purpose other than to allow him to emerge alive from that journey through the kingdom of the dead and permit him to see the light of day once more. During those moments, his consciousness registered no sensation but the diligent repetition of the mechanical, professional acts of soldiering. He was resigned to the inevitable, and that drove him forward; that and the fact that one comrade was in front of him and another followed at his heels. That was the place Fate had assigned him on this earth—or, to be more precise, beneath it— and nothing he could think or feel was going to change it. Absurd, therefore, to waste time and concentration on anything other than dragging himself along with his pistol in one hand and dagger in the other, and all for no reason but to repeat the macabre ritual men have repeated through the centuries: killing to stay alive. Beyond such beautiful simplicity, nothing had meaning. His king and his country—whatever the true country of Captain Alatriste might be—were too far away from that subterranean hell to matter, too far from that blackness at whose end he continued to hear, ever closer, the laments of the Dutch sappers who had been caught by the explosion. There was no doubt that Mendieta had reached them, because now Alatriste could hear muffled blows, the slicing and cracking of flesh and bones dealt by the short-handled spade which, according to the sounds, the Biscayan was swinging freely.

Beyond the rubble, the bones, and the dust, the caponniere widened into a larger space. It was the Dutch tunnel, now a scene of shadowy pandemonium. Still burning in a corner was the wick of a tallow lantern that was about to go out; it gave off a dim reddish light, barely enough to suggest the vague outlines of the shadows moaning nearby. Alatriste rolled out of the caponniere onto his knees, stuffed his pistol into his belt, and felt around with his free hand. Mendieta was wielding his spade without mercy, and a Dutch voice suddenly erupted in howls. Someone stumbled from the mouth of the caponniere onto the captain's back; he could hear his comrades arriving one after the other. A pistol shot briefly lit the area, revealing bodies dragging themselves across the ground or lying motionless. The same fleeting flash illuminated Mendieta's spade, red with blood.

A current of air from the depths of the Dutch tunnel was blowing dust and smoke toward the caponniere, and

Alatriste cautiously felt his way toward it. He bumped into something alive, alive enough that a Flemish curse preceded the flash of a shot that nearly blinded the captain and singed the hairs on his face. He lunged forward, grabbed his adversary, and slashed twice, up and across, meeting only air, and then another two slashes forward, the second finding flesh. He heard a scream and then the sound of a body scrabbling away; in a second, Alatriste was after him, guided by the fleeing man's cries of pain. He trapped him finally, catching him by the foot and drove his dagger from that foot upward, again and again, until his prey ceased to shout or move.

"*Ik geef mij over!*" someone wailed in the shadows.

That was out of place, for everyone knew that no prisoners were taken in the caponnieres, just as the Spaniards, when dealt a bad hand, expected no quarter. The voice soon gurgled in a death rattle when one of the attackers, guided by sound, reached the heretic and silenced him with his dagger. Alatriste heard more sounds of fighting and paused to listen, motionless and alert. There were two more shots, and in their flash, he saw Copons close by, locked in a struggle with a Hollander, rolling across the ground. Then he heard the Olivares brothers calling each other in low voices. Copons and the Dutchman were not making any noise, and for an instant the captain wondered who was alive and who not.

"Sebastián!" he whispered.

Copons answered with a grunt, clarifying any doubt. Now there was almost no sound except for a low moan here and there, some ragged breathing, and the scraping sound of men crawling across the tunnel floor. Alatriste moved forward again on his knees, one hand held before him, groping in the darkness, the other tense and ready by his side, clutching his dagger. The last sputter of the lantern showed that the mouth of the tunnel leading to the enemy trenches was filled with rubble and splintered wood. A body lay sprawled there, motionless, and after striking twice with his dagger to be sure, the Captain crawled over it toward the tunnel. He paused a few instants, listening. There was nothing but silence on the other side, but he caught an odor.

"Sulfur!" he yelled.

The toxic cloud moved slowly down the tunnel, undoubtedly propelled by bellows the Dutch were pumping in order to flood the passage with a haze of burnt straw, tar, and sulfur. They obviously did not have the welfare of any compatriots still alive in mind, or perhaps by that point they were convinced that no one could have survived. The current of air favored their operation, and in less time than it takes to recite an Our Father, the noxious smoke would have poisoned the air. With a sudden sense of urgency, Alatriste scrabbled back through the rubble and bodies, bumped into the comrades clogging the mouth of the caponniere, and finally, after what seemed like years, he was again pulling his body rapidly through fallen earth and remains from the cemetery. The grunts and curses of someone he thought was Garrote pressed him from behind. The captain passed beneath the opening in the ceiling of the caponniere, desperately gasped air from outside, and then continued along the tight passageway, lips pressed and breath held, until over the head of the comrade preceding him he saw light ahead, gradually growing brighter. At last he emerged into the large tunnel, which had been abandoned by the German sappers, and then fell into the Spanish trench. He ripped the kerchief from his mouth and frantically gulped air, then used the cloth to scrub the sweat and dirt from his face. All around him, like cadavers restored to life, were the wan, grimy faces of his comrades, exhausted and blinded by the light. Finally, once his eyes had adjusted, he saw Captain Bragado waiting with the German sappers and the rest of the group.

"Is everyone here?" Bragado asked.

Rivas and one of the Olivares were missing. Pablo, the younger one, his hair and beard no longer black but gray from powder and dirt, started toward the tunnel to look for his brother but was held back by Garrote and Mendieta. The Dutch, enraged by this turn of events, were now sending heavy fire our way from the other side, and musket balls whizzed past heads and bounced off the gabion baskets of the trench.

"Well, we really fucked them," said Mendieta.

There was no triumph in his tone, only profound weariness. He still had his spade in his hand, covered with clumps of blood and earth. Copons lay on the ground beside Alatriste, breathing with difficulty, his face covered with a shining mask of sweat and clay.

"Whoresons!" the younger of the Olivares shouted. "Heretic sons of beggars' bawds, may you roast in hell!"

His imprecations ceased as Rivas's head emerged from the mouth of the tunnel; he was dragging the other Olivares, half suffocated but still alive. The Galician's blue eyes were bloodshot.

"God a' mercy."

His blond hair was smoking with sulfur. He clawed the kerchief from his face, coughing up dirt.

"Thanks be to God," he said, filling his lungs with fresh air.

One of the Germans brought a small wineskin of water, and the men drank greedily, one after the other.

"Even if it were ass's piss," Garrote muttered, spilling water down his chin and chest.

Leaning against the trench wall and feeling Bragado's eyes on him, Alatriste cleaned the dirt and blood from his *vizcaína*.

"How is the tunnel?" the officer asked finally.

"Clean as this dagger."

Without another word Alatriste sheathed the weapon. Then he removed the primer charge from the pistol he had not needed to use.

"Thanks be to God," Rivas repeated over and over, crossing himself. His blue eyes wept black earth.

Alatriste said nothing aloud, but to himself he said, "Sometimes God seems to have had enough." Then, sickened with pain and blood, he gazed toward the other side and rested.

8. ATTACK BY NIGHT

In this way the month of April went by, rainy days alter-
nating with clear days. The grass grew greener in the fields
and trenches, and on the graves of the dead. Our canon battered the walls of Breda; the sapping of mines and countermines continued; and every good Christian made use of
his harquebus, skirmishing from trench to trench, with an
assault from us and a sortie from the Dutch occasionally
breaking the monotony of the siege. It was about that time
that we began to hear news of terrible shortages, a true
famine suffered by the besieged, although those of us doing
the besieging were worse off than they. But with this difference: They had been brought up in fertile lands, with
rivers and fields and cities regaled by Fortune; we
Spaniards had for centuries been watering ours with blood
and sweat just to get a scrap of bread. So, since our enemies

were fashioned more for pleasure rather than the lack of sustenance, some by nature and others by custom, a number of the English and French in Breda began to abandon their units and come over to our camp, telling us that behind those walls the deaths now numbered some five thousand, including common folk, burghers, and military. From time to time the dawn would see hanging before the walls of the city Dutch spies who had been attempting to deliver increasingly desperate letters between the head of the garrison, Justin of Nassau, and his relative Maurice, who was only a few leagues away and unyielding in his determination to rescue the stronghold by breaking a siege that was now nearing a year in length.

In those days, too, came news of a dike that the same Maurice of Nassau was constructing near Sevenberge, two hours' march from Breda, with the aim of diverting the waters of the Merck toward our camp in order, with the aid of the tides, to flood the Spanish barracks and trenches. Troops and provisions could also be brought to the city by boat. It was a grand, ambitious, and very timely enterprise. Also grand was the number of sappers and boatmen engaged in cutting sod and fascines for fortifications and in transporting stone, trees, and timber for its construction. They had already dug three anchorages lined with rubblework and were progressing from both sides, containing the mud with large wood retaining walls and securing the locks with pontoons and palisades. This news was a great worry to our General Spínola, who was seeking, without finding, an efficient way to prevent us waking in water up to our necks. On this point, it was said by way of jest, we would have to send men from the German *tercios* to thwart Nassau's project, because they were a nation that could lend their basic skills to the purpose:

He set that crew of Germans down
and then he said to them,
"The dike that you see there must go
or we will all be drowned."
And I am here to let you know
that as water was not their drink,
that dike vanished from his sight
'ere he'd had time to blink.

It was also during those days that Captain Alatriste received an order to present himself in the tent of Colonel don Pedro de la Daga. He went there late in the afternoon, as the sun was setting over the flat landscape bathing the banks of the dikes in a rosy glow and silhouetting the windmills and trees that stretched toward the swamps in the northwest. Alatriste had smartened himself up as much as he was able: His buffcoat hid his mended shirt; his weapons were burnished to an even brighter sheen; and his belts had been liberally treated with tallow. He entered the tent bareheaded, with his battered hat in one hand and the other resting on the pommel of his sword. He stood there, erect, not opening his mouth until don Pedro de la Daga, who was speaking with other officers, among them Captain Bragado, decided to grant him his attention.

"So here he is," said the colonel.

Alatriste showed neither uneasiness nor curiosity at the unusual summons, though his attentive eyes did not miss the discreet, calming smile that Bragado sent him from behind the colonel's back. There were four other officers in the tent, all of whom he knew by sight: don Hernán Torralba, captain of another of the *banderas*; Sergeant-Major Idiáquez; and two *guzmanes,* the two caballeros attached to de la Daga's military staff. Aristocrats and well-bred hidalgos often served without pay in the *tercios* for love of glory or, which was more common, to establish a reputation before returning to Spain to enjoy the sinecures that would be theirs through influence, friendships, and family. All the men were holding crystal wine goblets that had been filled from bottles on a table covered in books and maps. Alatriste had not seen a crystal goblet since the sacking of Oudkerk. A meeting of shepherds and wine, he said to himself, means one dead sheep.

"Would you care for a little, señor?"

The twist of Jiñalasoga's lips was meant to be amiable,

as he indicated the bottles and goblets with a casual sweep of his hand.

"It is good Pedro Ximénez wine," he added. "We've just received it from Málaga."

Alatriste swallowed hard, hoping that no one would notice. At noon in the trenches he and his comrades had feasted on a few sips of dirty water and bread seasoned with turnip oil. For that reason, he sighed: each to his own. It was in the long run more comfortable to keep one's distance from one's superiors, just as they were more comfortable keeping theirs from their inferiors.

"With Your Mercy's leave," he said after a moment's thought, "I will have some another time."

He had slightly adjusted his stance while speaking, as if to stand at attention, attempting to do so with the proper respect. Even so, the colonel arched an eyebrow and after an instant turned his back to him, ignoring him as if he were preoccupied with the maps on the table. The *guzmanes* looked Alatriste up and down with curiosity. As for Carmelo Bragado, who was standing in the background beside Captain Torralba, his smile had grown a little broader, but it disappeared when Sergeant-Major Idiáquez took center stage. Ramiro Idiáquez was a veteran with a gray mustache and white hair, which he wore cut very short. An old injury to his nose made it look as if it were slit at the tip, a reminder of the attack and sacking of

Calais at the end of the old century, in the days of our good king Philip the Second.

"We have received a challenge," he said with the brusqueness he used for giving orders and everything else. "Tomorrow morning. Five against five by the Den Bosh gate."

In those days such events were a normal part of an officer's duties. Not satisfied with the normal ebb and flow of the war, the antagonists sometimes took things to a personal level, with braggadocio and rodomontades in which the honor of nations and flags was at stake. Even the great Emperor Charles V, to the enjoyment of all Europe, had challenged his enemy Francis I of France to one-on-one combat; the Frenchman, however, and after a great deal of thought, had declined the offer. In the end, history had called in the French toad's chips when in Pavía he saw his troops demolished, the flower of his nobility annihilated, and he himself lying flat on the ground with the sword of Juan de Urbieta, a citizen of Hernani, resting on his royal gullet.

Then came a brief silence. Alatriste was impassive, hoping that someone would say something more. In the end, it was one of the *guzmanes* who spoke.

"Yesterday, two vain, self-satisfied Dutch caballeros from Breda came out to deliver the message. Apparently one of our harquebusiers killed a man of some importance in the trenches of the stronghold. They asked for one hour on open ground, five against five, each man carrying two pistols and a sword. Of course, the gauntlet was picked up."

"Of course!" the second *guzmán* repeated.

"Men from Campo Látaro's Italian *tercio* asked to participate, but it has been decided that we should all be Spanish."

"Only natural," put in the other.

Alatriste examined them very slowly. The first to have spoken appeared to be about thirty. He was wearing clothing that heralded his social position, and the baldric of his Toledo sword was of good Moroccan leather tooled in gold. For some reason, despite the war, he had elected to wear his mustache tightly curled. He was disagreeable and haughty. The second man, broader and shorter, was also younger. He affected a slightly Italian style, with a rich collar of Brussels lace and a short velvet doublet with sleeves slashed in satin. The identifying red band both men wore was edged with gold tassels, and their fine leather boots with spurs were very different from the boots Alatriste was wearing at that moment: His were wrapped in rags to keep his toes from peeping out. He could imagine those two enjoying their intimate acquaintance with the colonel, who in turn would, through them, strengthen his connections in Brussels and Madrid, all of them laughing and exchanging thank-yous and Your Mercies. Dogs trotting on

the same leash. He knew the name of the first only by reputation: don Carlos del Arco, a native of Burgos and son of
a marqués, or son of something. Alatriste had twice seen
him fight, and he was judged to be courageous.

"Don Luis de Bobadilla and I make two," don Carlos continued. "And we will need an additional three men with
livers, not lilies, so we will be on even terms."

"In truth we are lacking only one," Sergeant-Major
Idiáquez corrected. "To accompany these caballeros I have
already chosen Pedro Martín, a brave man from the *bandera* of Captain Gómez Coloma. And the fourth will prob-
ably be Eguiluz, from don Hernán Torralba's company."

"A good menu for serving Nassau a bad meal," the
guzmán concluded.

Alatriste digested all this in silence. He knew Martín
and Eguiluz, both veteran soldiers who could be trusted
when it came to shaking hands with the Dutch, or with
anyone else for that matter. Neither would make a bad
partner at the fiesta.

"You will be the fifth," said don Carlos del Arco.

Unblinking, with his hat in one hand and the other on
his sword, Alatriste frowned. He did not care for the
dandy's tone or the way he considered Alatriste's role a fait
accompli, especially since this *guzmán* was not exactly an

officer. Nor did he like the gold tassels on his red band or the petulant air of a man who has an endless supply of gold coins in his pouch and a father in Burgos who is a marqués. Finally, he did not like the fact that his commander, Captain Bragado, was standing there without a word to say for himself. Bragado was a good military man, and he knew how to combine those skills with delicate diplomacy, which had stood him in good stead during his career, but Diego Alatriste y Tenorio was not the kind of man to welcome orders from arrogant fops, however daring they might be and however much they drank his colonel's wine from crystal goblets. All of which caused the affirmative answer he was about to give to linger a moment on his lips. That hesitation was misinterpreted by del Arco.

"Of course," he said with a snort of disdain, "if you consider the matter too dangerous . . ."

He left his words hanging in the air and looked around, as a smirk appeared on his companion's face. Ignoring the warning glances Captain Bragado was sending his way, Alatriste took his hand from his sword and fingered his mustache with supreme calm. It was a way as good as any to contain the anger surging from his stomach to his chest, causing his blood to pound slowly, regularly, in his temples. He fixed his icy gaze on one of the caballeros and then on the other for a long moment, so long that the colonel, who had been standing all that time with his back turned, as if none of this concerned him, swung around to observe him. But Alatriste was already addressing Carmelo Bragado.

"I assume that this is your order, *mi capitán*."

Bragado slowly put his hand to the back of his neck, rubbing it without answering, and then looked toward Sergeant-Major Idiáquez, whose furious eyes were shooting daggers at the two *guzmanes*. But then don Pedro de la Daga himself replied.

"There are no orders in questions of honor," he said insolently. "Each man is answerable for his reputation and his shame."

When he heard that, Alatriste paled, and his right hand slowly descended toward the hilt of his blade. The look Bragado sent him was now imploring: to show even an inch of blade would mean the gallows. But Alatriste was thinking of something more than an inch. In fact, he was coolly calculating how much time he would need to thrust the sword through the colonel first and then quickly turn to the caballeros. Perhaps he would have time to take one of them, preferably Carlos del Arco, before Idiáquez and Bragado killed him like a dog.

The sergeant-major cleared his throat, visibly perturbed. He was the only person who, because of his rank and privileges in the *tercio*, could contradict Jiñalasoga. He had also known Diego Alatriste some twenty years, ever since that day in Amiens when, one being a boy and the other a youth whose mustache was just beginning to grow, they had set out together from the Montrecourt ravelin in the company of Captain don Diego de Villalobos: In four hours they had nailed down the enemy artillery and killed the last of the eight-hundred Frenchmen manning the trenches, giving in exchange the lives of seventy comrades. Which was not a bad trade, *pardiez*: eleven of them for every one of us, if my arithmetic is correct, and a bonus of thirty.

"With all due respect, Your Mercy," Idiáquez intervened, "Diego Alatriste is a veteran soldier. Everyone knows that his reputation is irreproachable. I am sure that . . ."

The colonel interrupted him with a curt gesture. "Irreproachable reputations are not granted for life."

"Diego Alatriste is a good soldier," Captain Bragado spoke up from the background; he had become embarrassed by his own silence.

Don Pedro de la Dago quieted him with another brusque gesture. "Any good soldier—and in *my tercio* they are as numerous as grains of sand—would give his arm to be at the Den Bosh gate tomorrow morning."

Diego Alatriste looked straight into the colonel's eyes. His voice was slow and low, as cold as the fingertips tingling to draw his dagger.

"I use my two arms to comply with my duty to the king.

He is the one who pays me . . . when I am paid." His pause seemed infinitely long. "As for my honor and my reputation, have no care, Your Mercy, for I see to that, with no need for anyone to offer me duels or give me lessons."

The colonel looked at Alatriste as if he intended to remember him for the rest of his life. It was clear that he was reviewing in his mind everything he had heard, sentence by sentence, seeking one word, a tone, a nuance, that would allow him to string a rope in the nearest tree. This was so obvious that the hand covered by Alatriste's hat slid toward his left hip, close to the hilt of his dagger. At the first sign, he thought with resigned calm, I will put this dagger through your throat, pull out my sword, and let God or the devil prevail.

"This man may return to the trenches," Jiñalasoga said finally.

No doubt the memory of the recent mutiny tempered the colonel's natural inclination to make use of the noose. Bragado and Idiáquez, who had been watching Diego Alatriste's hands, seemed to relax with no little relief. Cloaking the relief that he too was feeling, Alatriste nodded respectfully, turned, and walked from the tent into the fresh air, pausing beside the halberds of the German sentinels who could, so easily, have been leading him on a scenic trip to the gallows. He stood stock-still for a moment, gratefully observing a sun that was disappearing below the dikes, a sun that he was now certain of seeing rise the next morning. Then he clapped his hat onto his head and started back to the parapets leading to The Cemetery ravelin.

That night Captain Alatriste, wrapped in his cape, lay awake almost till dawn, gazing up at the stars. It was neither the colonel's disfavor nor fear of dishonor that kept him awake while his comrades snored around him. He did not give a fig for whatever version of the story might circulate through the *tercio,* for Idiáquez and Bragado knew him well and would give the episode the report it deserved. Furthermore, as he had said to don Pedro de la Daga, he would earn his own respect among his equals as well as those who were not. No, it was something else that denied him sleep. And that something was his fervent wish that at least one of the *guzmanes* would survive the next day at the Den Bosh gate. Preferably Carlos del Arco. For then, he told himself as his eyes drank in the firmament, time passes, life takes many turns, and a man never knows what old acquaintance he might meet in just the right place, at just the right time: in the quiet darkness, with no one around to hear the sound of ringing swords.

The next day, with our men watching from our trenches and the enemy from theirs as well as from atop the city walls, five men walked forward from the lines of our lord and king toward the encounter while another five emerged from the Den Bosh gate. These five, according to the rumor running around the camp, were three Dutchmen, a Scot, and a Frenchman. As for ours, Captain Bragado had chosen as the fifth member of the party Second Lieutenant Minaya, a thirty-year-old from the city of Soria: honorable, trustworthy, with good legs and a better hand. Both teams came wearing a sword and two pistols at the waist but no dagger; it was said that the challengers had not included them because everyone knows how dangerous a Spaniard with a dagger can be in close combat.

I had returned the previous night from three days of foraging—which had taken me, along with a crew of *mochileros*, almost to the banks of the Mosa—and now I was standing in the crowd with my friend Jaime Correas on top of some gabions, for once unafraid of being struck by a musket ball. Hundreds of soldiers were watching from every quarter, and it was rumored that the Marqués de los Balbases, our General Spínola, was himself observing the challenge in the company of don Pedro de la Daga and the captains and colonels of the remaining *tercios*. As for Diego Alatriste, he was in one of the forward trenches with Copons, Garrote, and others from his squad, with very little to say but with his eyes firmly fixed on the antagonists. Second Lieutenant Minaya, no doubt informed by our Captain Bragado, had done something that was the act of a good comrade: He had come by earlier that morning and asked to borrow one of Alatriste's pistols, using the pretext that he had some problem with his, and now he was walking to the fight with that pistol at his waist. It said a great deal in his favor and prevented acrimony within the *bandera*. I will add here that many years later, after Rocroi, when the vagaries of fortune had made me an officer in the Spanish guard of King Philip, our lord and king, I had occasion to do a favor for a young recruit named Minaya. I did so without a moment's hesitation, remembering the day when his father had the good grace to wear Captain Alatriste's pistol as he went to the encounter below the walls of Breda.

So there they were that April morning, with a warm sun overhead and thousands of eyes focused on them: five against five. They met in a small meadow that sloped down about a hundred paces toward the Den Bosh gate in no man's land. There were no preliminaries, no doffing of hats or other courtesies. Instead, as one group neared the other they began to fire and to draw their swords, at which both camps of watchers, who had until that instant observed in mortal silence, burst into a clamor of encouraging cries to their respective comrades. I know that from the beginning of time, well-intentioned people have condemned violence and preached peace and God's word, and

I, better than many, know what war does to a man's body and soul, but despite all that, despite my capacity to reason, despite my common sense and the lucidity lent by years, I cannot help but shiver with admiration when I witness the courage of valiant men. And God knows those men were.

Don Luis de Bobadilla, the younger of the two *guzmanes*, went down with the first shots, while the others closed in on each other with great energy and deadly intent. One of the Dutchmen was felled by a pistol shot that broke his neck, and another of his companions, the Scot, was wounded in the torso, run through by the sword of Pedro Martín, who lost it there. Finding himself with no sword and two discharged pistols, he was then knifed in the throat and chest, falling upon the man he had just killed. As for don Carlos del Arco, he engaged the Frenchman so skillfully that, between thrust and counter thrust, he was able to aim a shot at his face, though he then withdrew from the fight, hobbled by a wicked wound to his thigh. Minaya finished off the Frenchman with Captain Alatriste's pistol and badly wounded the second Dutchman with his own, emerging without a scratch himself. And Eguiluz, his left hand crippled by a musket ball but with his sword in his right, dealt two clean blows to the last of their opponents, one on an arm and the other to the flank. The heretic, seeing himself wounded and alone, resolved, like Antigone, not to flee exactly, but to fall back and check his resources. The three Spaniards still standing relieved their adversaries of their weapons and their bands, which were orange, according to the custom of those who served the Estates General. They would even have carried the bodies of Bobadilla and Martín to our lines had the Dutch, furious at the outcome, not consoled themselves over their defeat with a hailstorm of musket balls. Our men, therefore, were slowly quitting the field when a musketeer's lead struck Eguiluz in the kidneys, and although, helped by his companions, he reached the trenches, he died three days later. As for the seven bodies, they lay on open ground almost all day, until there was a brief truce at dusk and each side was able to recover its own.

No one in the *tercio* questioned Captain Alatriste's honor. The proof was that a week later, when the decision was made to attack the Sevenberge dike, he and his squad were among the forty-four men chosen for the task. They left our position at sunset, taking advantage of the first night of heavy fog to conceal their movements. They were under the command of Captains Bragado and Torralba, and they all wore their shirts on the outside of their doublets and buffcoats, in order to recognize one another in the dark. This was common practice among Spanish troops as well as the origin of the term *encamisadas*, being "shirted," given to night maneuvers. This attack was designed to capitalize on the natural aggressiveness and skill of our men in hand-to-hand combat: infiltrate a heretic camp, catch them unawares, kill as many as possible, burn their barracks and tents—though only when they were about to retire, to prevent providing unnecessary light—and get out at top speed. The troops were carefully chosen, and among Spaniards it was considered an honor to participate in an *encamisada*, so much so that often there were squabbles among the soldiers who wanted to be one of the party, as it was a bitter affront not to be included. The rules were strict, and customarily the execution of the raid was extremely well disciplined, in order to save lives in the confusion of the night. Of those undertaken in Flanders, the one at Mons was famous: five-hundred Germans under salary of the House of Orange dead, their camp burnt to ashes. In another, fifty were chosen to carry out the night foray, but when the appointed hour came, soldiers arrived from every direction, claiming to have been selected. When finally they did set off, instead of the usual silence, there were boisterous arguments in the middle of the night, more like a Moorish raid than a Spanish *encamisada*, with three hundred men racing along the road, trying to reach the goal ahead of their comrades. The enemy awoke to see coming toward them a swell of maddened, yelling demons in white shirts, slaughtering indiscriminately and brawling among themselves, competing to see who could kill better and more.

But as for Sevenberge, our General Spínola's plan was to travel the two long hours to the dike with great stealth and silence, surprise those guarding it, and destroy the work, breaching the locks with axes and burning everything in sight. It had been decided that a half dozen of us *mochileros* would be needed to carry the equipment for the fire and the sapping. So that night saw me in the line of Spaniards marching along the right bank of the Merck, where the fog was thickest. In the hazy darkness all you could hear was the muffled sound of footsteps—we were wearing espadrilles or boots wrapped in rags, and we knew we would pay with our lives if we were to speak aloud, light a cord, prime pistols or harquebuses—and the white shirts moved through the night like ghostly shrouds. Some time before, I had been forced to sell my beautiful Solingen, for we *mochileros* were not allowed to carry a sword, so I had only my dagger snugged into my belt. But I was not, *pardiez*, short of a load: the large pouch over my shoulders was packed with charges of powder and sulfur wrapped in petards, garlands of pitch to set the fires, and two sharpened hatchets for splintering the wood of the locks.

I was trembling with cold despite the coarse wool jerkin I was wearing beneath my shirt, which looked white only at night and had more holes in it than a flute. The fog created an unreal atmosphere around us, soaking my hair and dribbling down my face as if it were fine rain or the *chirimiri* of my homeland, making everything slippery and causing me to walk with great care, for if I slipped on the wet grass it would mean tumbling into the cold waters of the Merck with ballast of sixty pounds on my back. The night and the misty air allowed me to see about as far as a fried flounder might: two or three vague white splotches before me and two or three behind. The closest soldier, whose progress I was diligently following, was Captain Alatriste. His squad was in the vanguard, preceded only by Captain Bragado and two Walloon guides from the Soest *tercio,* or what remained of it, whose mission, apart from acting as guides since they knew this region well, consisted of outwitting the Dutch sentinels and getting close enough to cut their throats before they had time to sound the alarm. To do that they had chosen a route that entered enemy territory after passing between large swamps and peat bogs and along very narrow paths that often became dikes where men could walk only in single file.

We crossed over to the side of the river by means of a palisade-reinforced pontoon bridge that led to a dike separating the left bank from the swamps. The white blur of Captain Alatriste moved on in silence, as always. I had watched him slowly equip himself at sunset: buffcoat beneath his shirt and outside it the large belt with sword, dagger, and the pistol Second Lieutenant Minaya had returned to him, its pan well greased to protect it from the wet. He also tied to his belt a small flask of powder, a pouch with ten musket balls, and spare flint, tinder, and steel, should they be needed. Before tying on the powder, he had checked its color, not too black or too gray; its grain, which was hard and fine; and touched a little to his tongue to test the saltpeter. Then he had asked Copons for his whet stone and spent a long time sharpening both edges of his dagger. Those in the lead, which was his group, were not carrying harquebuses or muskets, for the first assault would be made with blades until the site was secured for their comrades. For that task it was best to be lightly armed, with hands free of encumbrance. The quartermaster of our *bandera* had asked for young and able *mochileros*, and Jaime Correas and I had volunteered, reminding him that we had already performed well in the surprise attack at Oudkerk. When Captain Alatriste saw me with my shirt on the outside and my dagger in my belt, he had not said that it seemed a good idea to him, but then again, he had not said it didn't. All he did was nod and point to one of the packs. Then, in the misty light of the bonfires, we all knelt, prayed an Our Father in a murmur that ran down the rows, crossed ourselves, and started off toward the northwest.

The line suddenly stopped, and the men crouched down and in low voices sent back the password, which Captain

Bragado had decided only then: *Antwerp.* Everything had been so well planned before we left that without need for orders or commentary, a succession of white shirts now filed past me, dividing to the left and right. I heard the splashing of men along both sides of the dike, wading in water up to their waists, and the soldier behind me touched my shoulder and took the pack. His face was a dark blur, and I could hear his agitated breathing as he fastened the straps and continued forward. When I turned back and looked ahead, Captain Alatriste's shirt had disappeared into the darkness and the fog. Now the last shadows passed me by, fading away with the muted sounds of steel being drawn from sheaths and the soft *chink chink* of harquebuses and pistols finally being loaded and primed. I went a few steps farther with them, and then I lay face down on the edge of the slope, on the wet grass where the soldiers' footsteps had churned up mud. Someone crawled up beside me from behind. It was Jaime Correas, and the two of us stayed there, talking in whispers, staring anxiously into the darkness that had swallowed forty-four Spaniards who meant to give the heretics a bad night.

About the time it took for two rosaries passed by. My comrade and I were numb with cold, and we pressed close to share our warmth. We could hear nothing but the water running along the side of the dike leading to the river.

"They're taking a long time," Jaime whispered.

I did not answer. At that moment I was thinking of Captain Alatriste in cold water up to his chest, pistol held high to keep the powder dry, a dagger or sword in the other hand, creeping up on the Dutch sentinels guarding the locks. Then I thought of Caridad la Lebrijana and ended up thinking about Angélica de Alquézar as well. Often, I told myself, women do not know what perfection and perdition lie in the hearts of men.

A harquebus shot rang out: only one, distant, isolated, in the night and fog. I estimated it to be more than three hundred paces before us, and we flattened ourselves against the slope even more. The silence returned for an instant, and then a furious succession of shots rang out, pistols and muskets. On edge, feverish from the uproar, Jaime and I tried to peer into the dark but to no avail. Now the firing was coming from both directions, growing louder and more frequent, reverberating across sky and earth as if a storm were discharging its thunder and lightning under the cover of darkness. There was a sharp, loud report, and two more followed. Then we could see that the fog was lifting a little: A pale, milky, then reddish glow grew, diffusing itself in the tiny droplets that filled the air and were reflected in the dark water below the slope where we lay. The Sevenberge dike was aflame.

I never knew how much time had passed, but I do know that in the distance the night was roaring like hell itself.

Finally we sat up a little, fascinated, and at that moment we heard the sound of steps running toward us down the dike. Finally, a succession of white blurs, shirts racing through the darkness, began to take shape through the fog, passing us and heading in the direction of the Spanish camp. The eruptions of shots continued from the harquebuses ahead of us as the pale silhouettes continued to run past, with the sound of footsteps sloshing through mud, oaths, ragged breathing, and the moan of someone wounded being helped along by his comrades. Now the crack of muskets was coming closer, and the white shirts, which had at first arrived in clusters, were beginning to thin out.

"Let's go," said Jaime, jumping up and breaking into a run.

I in turn sprang up, spurred by a wave of panic. I did not want to be left behind, alone. A few stragglers were still passing us, and in each white splotch I tried to make out the silhouette of Captain Alatriste. One shadow was staggering along the dike, running with difficulty, its breathing choked by the moan of pain that escaped with each step. Before the figure reached me it fell and rolled down the slope, and I heard it splash into the water. Without thinking, I jumped down the slope after it, into water up to my knees, feeling through the dark until I touched a motionless body. I felt a corselet beneath the shirt and a bearded face, icy as death itself. It was not the captain.

Shots roared closer with every minute. They seemed to be coming from every direction. I stumbled up the slope to the top of the dike, disoriented, and I realized that I had lost a sense of which was the good side and which the bad. I could no longer see the red glow in the distance, and no one was running past me any more. Nor could I remember which direction the man who had fallen down had come from or determine in which direction to run. My head was filled with a silent scream of panic. Think! I told myself. Think calmly, Íñigo Balboa, or you will never see the dawn. I knelt on one knee, forcing my reason to tame the wild beating of blood at my temples. The soldier had fallen into quiet water, I remembered. And then I realized that I was hearing the soft sound of the Merck flowing at the bottom of the slope on my right. The river flows toward Sevenberge, I reasoned. And we had come along the right bank, crossing to the left over the pontoon bridge. I was, therefore, facing in the wrong direction. So I turned and began to run, cleaving the dark night as if instead of Hollanders I had the very devil behind me.

I have run like that only a few times in my life. Your Mercies should try it, soaked in water and mud in the black of night. I ran blindly, with my head down, risking a roll down the slope straight into the Merck. As the cold, moist air entered my lungs it turned to fire, and I felt as if my chest were being pricked by red-hot needles. Then, just as I was beginning to wonder if I had gone too far, I came to the pontoons. I grabbed onto the stakes and concentrated on crossing, slipping on the wet wood. I had barely reached the other side, back on solid ground, when a flash lit the darkness and the whirr of a harquebus ball passed a hair's breadth from my head.

"Antwerp!" I yelled, throwing myself to the ground.

"Bugger it," a voice replied.

Two pale silhouettes, crouched down, were outlined against the fog.

"You've just had a lucky escape, comrade," said the second voice.

I got to my feet and went toward them. I could not see their faces, but I did see the white of their shirts and the sinister shadow of the harquebuses that had been so close to sending me to my rest:

"Did Your Mercies not see my shirt?" I asked, still breathless from running and fright.

"What shirt?" one asked.

I felt my chest, surprised, and did not swear only because I was still not old enough, nor was I in the habit of doing so. During the attack, I had lain face down for so long on the dike, my shirt was now dark with mud.

9. THE COLONEL AND THE BANNER

During that time, Maurice of Nassau died, to the sorrow of the Estates General and the gratification of the true religion, but not before wresting from us, by way of farewell, the city of Goch, burning the supplies we had stored in Ginneken and attempting to take Antwerp with a surprise attack that ended up backfiring on him. That heretic, the paladin of Calvin's abominable sect, would go to hell without allaying his obsessive hunger to end the siege of Breda. To offer our condolences to the Dutch, our cannons spent the day tidily dropping seventy-pound balls on the walls of the city, and at daybreak, through the efforts of our sappers, we blew up a bulwark with thirty good citizens inside, giving them a rather rude awakening and demonstrating that God does not always reward the early riser.

At that point Breda was no longer a matter of military interest to Spain but, rather, one of reputation. The world was in suspense, awaiting the triumph or failure of the troops of the Catholic king. Even the sultan of the Turks—may Christ visit foul excrescences upon him— was awaiting the outcome to see whether our lord and king would emerge with more or less power. And in Europe the eyes of every king and prince, particularly those of France and England, were focused on the stalemate, eager to benefit from our misfortune or to grieve over Spanish gain, which was equally true in the Mediterranean of the Venetians and even the Roman pope. For His Holiness, despite being the Divinity's earthly vicar, with all the attendant paraphernalia, and also despite the fact that it was we Spanish who were doing his dirty work in Europe, bankrupting ourselves in defense of God and the Most Blessed Mary, harassed us whenever he could, because he was jealous of our influence in Italy. There is nothing like being powerful and feared for a couple of centuries to cause enemies with malicious intentions, whether or not they wear the pope's triple crown, to spring up on every side. Under the mantle of pleasant words, smiles, and diplomacy, they take painstaking care in completely buggering you. Although in the case of the sovereign pontiff, his biliousness was, to a degree, understandable. After all, only a century before the problem of

Breda, his predecessor, Clement VII, had had to take to his heels, tucking up his cassock as he ran and taking refuge in the Castel SantAngelo, when the Spaniards and German mercenaries of our Charles V—who had carried an unpaid bill since the time of el Cid—had attacked his walls and sacked Rome without respecting cardinals' palaces, or women, or convents. It is therefore only fair we should remember that even popes have a good memory and their own crumb of honor.

"I have a letter for you, Íñigo."

Surprised, I looked up at Captain Alatriste. He was standing at the entrance to the hut we had constructed of blankets, fascines, and mud, where I was spending time with some of my comrades. He was wearing his hat and had thrown his frayed wool cape around his shoulders, its hem slightly lifted by the sheath of his sword. The broad brim of his hat, the heavy mustache and aquiline nose, accentuated the leanness of his weathered face, now unnaturally pale. He had not been in good health for several days, due to some foul water—our bread was moldy as well, and meat, when we had it, was full of worms—that had set his body on fire and poisoned his blood with fever. The captain, nonetheless, was no friend to bloodletting or purges; he always said those measures killed more often than they cured. So he was just returning from the camp of the sutlers, where an acquaintance who acted as both barber and apothecary had brewed a concoction of herbs to lower his fever.

"A letter for me?"

"So it seems."

I left Jaime Correas and the others and, brushing the dirt from my breeches, went outside. We were far out of range of the walls, near the palisade where we kept the carts and dray horses, and close to certain ramshackle hovels that served as taverns when there was wine, and as brothels with German, Italian, Flemish, and Spanish women for the troops. It was a favorite place for us *mochileros* to forage for food, with all the cunning and mischief our calling and our youth lent us as we sought ways to live in comparative comfort. It was rare that we did not return from our pilfering with two or three eggs, some apples, tallow candles, or some useful object we could sell or trade. With such industry I offered some succor to Captain Alatriste and his comrades, and when I had a real stroke of luck I bowed to my own pleasure, which might include a visit, along with Jaime Correas, to La Mendoza's shack, where, since the conversation between Diego Alatriste and the Valencian Candau on the banks of the dike, my entry had never been disputed. The captain, who knew what I was about, had discreetly admonished me, saying simply that women who follow soldiers are the source of pustules, pestilence, and sword fights. The truth is that I did not know what the captain's relations with such females had been in other times, but I can say that never in Flanders did I see him enter a house or a tent with a swan swinging at the entrance. I did learn, it is true, that once or twice, with Captain Bragado's permission, he had gone to Oudkerk, which was now the garrison of a Burgundian *bandera*, to visit the Flemish woman I have spoken of elsewhere. It was rumored that on his last visit, Alatriste had exchanged harsh words with the husband, whose arse he had ended up kicking into the canal, and had even had to draw his sword when a pair of Burgundians tried to squeeze into a procession they'd not been invited to join. But since that time, he had not been back.

As for me, my sentiments regarding the captain were beginning to be ambiguous, although I was barely aware of it. On the one hand, I obeyed him implicitly, offering him the sincere devotion that Your Mercies know so well. On the other hand, like any youth growing out of his boyhood, I was beginning to feel the weight of his shadow. Flanders had catalyzed the transformations in me natural for a boy who lived among soldiers and who furthermore had had the opportunity to fight for his life, his reputation, and his king. Also, I had recently been troubled by questions that my master's silences no longer answered. All of this was making me consider the possibility of enlisting as a soldier, and although I was not yet old enough—it was rare at that time to serve if one was younger than seventeen or eighteen, which meant I would have to lie—somehow I thought that a turn of fortune might somehow facilitate my ambition. After all, Captain Alatriste himself had enlisted when he was barely fifteen, during the siege of Hulst. That had been during the famous exercise conceived to divert the enemy from a planned attack on the fort of La Estrella, when *mochileros*, pages, and every available servant had marched out armed with pikes, banners, and drums and paraded along a dike, tricking the enemy into taking them for replacement troops. The assault that followed was bloody; so bloody that most of the youths, finding themselves with weapons and their zeal kindled by the battle, ran to back up their masters, courageously jumping into the fire. Diego Alatriste, who at that time was a drummer in the *bandera* of Captain Pérez de Espila, went with them. Some, Alatriste among them, fought so bravely that Prince Albert, who was already governor of Flanders and was personally overseeing the siege, rewarded them by letting them enlist.

"It came this morning with the post from Spain."

I took the letter the captain was holding out to me. It

was written on fine paper; the seal was intact, and my name
was on the front:

Señor don Diego Alatriste Attention of Íñigo
Balboa* In the Bandera of Captain don Carmelo
Bragado, of the Cartagena Tercio* Military post
of Flanders*

My hands trembled as I turned over the envelope sealed
with the initials *A. de A.* Without a word, and feeling Alatriste's eyes on me, I slowly walked some distance away to
where the Germans' women were washing clothes by a narrow branch of the river. The Germans, like some Spaniards,
took as their women former whores who assuaged their desires and also relieved them of the misery of washing soldiers' clothing. In addition, some sold liquors, firewood,
tobacco, and pipes to those who needed them, and I have already written how in Breda I saw German women working
in the trenches to help their husbands. Near the makeshift
laundry, where a tree that had been felled and trimmed
for cutting firewood lay across a large rock, I sat, unable to
tear my eyes from those initials, incredulously holding
Angélica's letter in my hands. I knew that the captain was
watching me the whole time, so I waited for my heart to
stop pounding and then, trying not to reveal my impatience,
I broke the seal and unfolded the letter.

Señor don Íñigo:

I have had notice of your pursuits, and I am pleased to know that you are serving in Flanders. Believe me when I say that I envy you for that.

I hope the rancor you hold for me over the difficulties you must have suffered following our last meeting is not too great. After all, I did one day hear you say that you would die for me. Take it therefore as one of life's tests, and remember that along with the bad times life can also offer satisfactions such as serving our lord and king or, perhaps, receiving this letter of mine.

I must confess that I cannot help but recall you every time I pass by the Acero fountain. However, I understand that you lost the handsome amulet I gave you there—something unpardonable in such an accomplished gallant as yourself.

I hope to see you someday here at court bedecked in sword and spurs. Until then, count on my memory and my smile.

Angélica de Alquézar

P.S. I rejoice that you are still alive. I have plans for you.

I had finished reading the letter—I read it three times, passing from stupor to happiness, and then to melancholy—

and had sat for a long time staring at the folded paper lying on the thick patches that repaired the knees of my breeches. I was in Flanders, at war, and she was thinking of me. There will be occasion—should I still have the desire, and the life, to continue recounting to Your Mercies the adventures of Captain Alatriste as well as my own—to detail the plans Angélica de Alquézar had for my person in that twenty-fifth year of the century, she being twelve or thirteen years old at the time and I on the road to fifteen. Plans that, had I divined them, would have made me tremble with both terror and delirium. I shall tell you here only that her beautiful and evil little head, graced with blue eyes and blonde curls, would—for some obscure reason that can be explained only by the secrets that certain women hold in the depths of their souls from the time they are young girls—place my neck and my eternal salvation in peril many times in the future. And she would always do it in the same contradictory manner: coldly and deliberately. Yet I believe that at the same time she sought my misfortune, she also loved me. And that was how it would be until she was taken from me—or until I freed myself from her, God mend me, nor am I sure which was the case—by her early and tragic death.

"I wonder if you have something to tell me," said Captain Alatriste.

He had spoken very softly, with nothing nuanced in his tone. I looked up. He was sitting beside me on the large rock beneath the tree. He held his hat in his hand and was staring with an absent air toward the distant walls of Breda.

"There is not much to say," I replied.

He nodded slowly, as if accepting what I said, and lightly stroked his mustache. Silence. His motionless profile made me think of a dark eagle resting high on a cliff. I noted the two scars on his face—one on an eyebrow and the other on his forehead—and the one on the back of his left hand, a memento Gualterio Malatesta had bestowed at the Las Animas gate. There were more scars hidden beneath his clothing, eight in total. I looked at the burnished hilt of his sword, the cobbled boots tied around his legs with harquebus cords, the rags visible through the holes in the soles, the mended tears in his threadbare brown cape. Perhaps, I thought, he had once been in love. Perhaps, in his way, he still was, and that included Caridad la Lebrijana and the silent blond Flemish woman in Oudkerk.

I heard him sigh softly, barely a breath expelled from his lungs, and then he made a move to get to his feet. I handed him the letter. He took it without a word and looked at me closely before he started reading, and now it was I who stared at the distant walls of Breda, as expressionless as he had been a moment before. Out of the corner of my eye I watched the hand with the scar rise to stroke his mustache again. Then he read. Finally I heard the crackle of the paper as he folded it, and once again I held the letter in my hands.

"There are things . . ." he began after a moment.

Then he stopped, and I thought that was all he would say, which would not have been strange in a man given more to silences than to words.

"Things," he continued finally, "that they know from the time they are born. Though they are not even aware that they know them."

Again he cut himself short. I heard him shifting uncomfortably, seeking a way to finish.

"Things it takes us men a lifetime to learn."

Then silence again, and this time he did not say anything more. Nothing in the vein of "Take care; guard against our enemy's niece," or other comments that one might have expected under the circumstances, and that I, as he undoubtedly knew, would have immediately ignored with all the arrogance of insolent youth. For a while he stared at the distant city, then put on his hat and stood up, settling his cape over his shoulders. And as I sat and watched him on his way back to the trenches, I wondered how many women, how many wounds, how many roads, and how many deaths—some owed to others and some to oneself—a man must know for those words to remain unspoken.

It was mid-May when Henry of Nassau, Maurice's successor, tried to test Fortune one last time, attempting to deliver Breda and to leave our bollocks buried in the ashes. It was the whim of fate that at that time, just on the eve of the day chosen by the Hollanders for their attack, our colonel and some of his staff were making a round of inspections along the northwest dikes and that Captain Alatriste's squad, chosen that week for the duty, was serving as escort. Don Pedro de la Daga was traveling with his usual ostentation: he and a half-dozen others on horseback with his commander-of-the-*tercio* standard, six Germans with halberds, and a dozen soldiers, among them Alatriste, Copons, and other comrades on foot, harquebuses and muskets shouldered, clearing the way for the general's party. I was bringing up the rear, carrying my pack filled with provisions and a supply of powder and balls, looking at the reflection of the string of men and horses in the quiet water of the canals, which the sun was tinting even more red as it sank toward the horizon. It was a peaceful dusk, with a clear sky and pleasant temperature; nothing seemed to announce the events that were about to be unleashed.

There had been movement of Dutch troops in the area, and don Pedro de la Daga had orders from General Spínola to take a look at the Italian positions near the Merck river, on the narrow road of the Sevenberge and

Strudenberge dikes, to ascertain whether they needed to be reinforced with a *bandera* of Spaniards. Jiñalasoga's intention was to stop for the night at the Terheyden garrison, which was under the command of the sergeant major of Campo Látaro's *tercio*, don Carlos Roma, and to devote the next day to making the necessary arrangements. We arrived at the dikes and the Terheyden fort before sunset, and everything seemed to be going as planned. Our colonel and his officers were lodged in the tents that had been prepared for them, while we were assigned to a small redoubt of wood stakes and gabions beneath the stars, where we wrapped ourselves in our capes after the meager mouthful the Italians, good and happy comrades, offered on our arrival. Captain Alatriste went to the colonel's tent to inquire if he might offer some service, and don Pedro de la Daga, with his usual disdain, replied that he had no need of him and that he should do as he wished. Upon the captain's return, as we were in a place unknown to us and there were both honorable and trustworthy men within Látaro's contingent, he decided that with the Italians or without them we should set up a guard. And so Mendieta was chosen for the first watch, one of the Olivares for the second, and Alatriste kept the third for himself. Mendieta, therefore, took his place close to the fire, his harquebus primed and cord lit, while the rest of us lay down to sleep any which way we could.

Dawn was breaking when I was awakened by strange noises and voices calling *To arms*! I opened my eyes to a dirty gray morning, to find Alatriste and the others moving around me, all heavily armed, lighting the slow matches of their harquebuses, filling powder pans, and ramming lead into muzzles as fast as they could. Close by I heard a deafening eruption of harquebuses and muskets and, amid the confusion, voices in the tongues of every nation. We later learned that Henry of Nassau had sent his English musketeers, all handpicked, and two hundred *coseletes* along the narrow dike. At their head was their English colonel, named Ver, who was also supported by French and German troops, his whole force numbering some six thousand, and all of them preceding a Dutch rear guard of heavy artillery, carriages, and cavalry. At first light the English had fallen upon the first Italian redoubt, which was defended by one lieutenant and a small contingent of soldiers, some of whom they blew out with grenades, killing the rest with their swords. Then they had placed harquebusiers in the protection of the redoubt, and with the same felicity and daring had taken the demilune in front of the gate of the fort, scaling the wall by hand and foot. When the Italians defending the trenches saw how far the enemy had advanced and their lack of cover on that side, they threw the handle after the ax head and vacated their position. The English fought with great vigor and honor—there was nothing lacking in their courage—so much so that the Italian company of Captain Camilo Fenice, who had come to defend the fort, saw themselves in a tight situation and turned their backs, with no little shame. Perhaps to make true what Tirso de Molina had said about certain soldiers.

Mutter thirteen curses,
sputter thirty 'Pon my lifes,
in cards harass the winners,
gather in wanton wives;
and in skirmishes and battles,
or in any grave disputes,
all the enemy will see of me
is the bottom of my boots.

It was not with verses but straightforward prose that the English reached the tents where our colonel and his officers had spent the night. They found them all outside in their nightshirts, armed however God allowed, fighting with swords and pistols in the midst of fleeing Italians and arriving English. From where we stood, some hundred paces from the tents, we watched the disorderly flight of the Italians and the throngs of English troops, all etched upon the gray dawn in flashes of powder. Diego Alatriste's first impulse was to lead his squad to the tents, but as soon as he stepped up on the parapet he realized that that would be fruitless, for the Italians were fleeing down the dike and no one was running toward us because there was no way out: At our backs was a small earthen elevation and behind it, swampy water. Only don Pedro de la Daga, his officers, and his German escort were making for our redoubt, battling their way, facing, not turning away from, the enemy, who was cutting off access to the retreat others were so vigorously pursuing. All this while, Lieutenant Miguel Chacón was attempting to protect our standard. When Alatriste saw that the small group was trying to reach our position, he lined up his men behind gabions and ordered them to fire continuously and protect de la Daga's withdrawal, and he himself loaded his harquebus and took shot after shot. I was squatting behind the parapet, hurrying to supply powder and musket balls when I was called.

Now, masses of enemies were upon us, and Lieutenant Chacón was running up the small incline before us when a ball struck him in the back, and he dropped where he was. We could see his bearded face, the gray hair of a veteran soldier, and watched as his clumsy fingers reached for the pole of the standard he had lost as he fell. He succeeded in grasping it and was struggling to his feet when a second shot tumbled him face up. Our standard lay crumpled on the ground beside the corpse of the lieutenant who had fulfilled his duty so honorably. Suddenly Rivas leaped from behind the gabions and ran toward the standard. I have already told Your Mercies that Rivas was from Finisterre, which is like saying the very ends of the earth; he was, *pardiez*, the last man anyone would have imagined leaving the parapet to retrieve a flag that he could take or leave. But with Galicians one never knows, and there are always men who surprise you. Well, there went our good Rivas, as I was saying, and he was halfway down the incline before he was struck by several musket balls and rolled down the terreplein almost to the feet of don Pedro de la Daga and his officers, who were being battered without mercy by the wave of attackers. The six Germans performing their obligations without imagination or complication as men do when they are well paid, were killed as God would have it, surrounding their colonel and selling their hides dear. The colonel had had time to buckle on his breastplate, which was the only reason he was still on his feet, though by now he had two or three serious wounds. The English kept coming, shouting, sure of their endeavor; the standard lying halfway down the slope merely fortified their daring, for a captured standard meant fame for the one who won it and shame for the one who lost it. That bit of checked blue-and-white cloth with a red band represented—in a sacrosanct tradition—the honor of Spain and of our lord and king.

"No quarter! No quarter!" the whoresons shouted.

Our fire had downed several of them, but by that point there was nothing that could save don Pedro de la Daga and his officers. One of them, unrecognizable because his face had been cut to ribbons, was trying to hold off the English so the colonel could escape. In all justice, I have to say that Jiñalasoga was faithful to himself to the end. Swatting away the officer who was tugging at his elbow and urging him to climb the hill, he left his sword in the body of one Englishman, blasted the face of another with his pistol, and then, neither ducking nor cringing—as arrogant on the road to hell as he had been in life—he gave himself to the blades of a pack of Englishmen who had recognized his rank and were competing for the spoils.

"No quarter! . . . No quarter!"

Only two of our officers were left alive, and they ran up the terreplein, taking advantage of the fact that the attackers were too busy feeding on the colonel. One died after a few steps, skewered by a pike. The other, the one with the badly cut face, staggered forward toward the standard, bent to pick it up, stood, and even managed to take three or four steps before he fell, riddled with pistol and musket balls. Again the standard was on the ground, but now no one was focusing on it; we were all too occupied

spraying harquebus balls at the English, who were nearing
the top of the slope above us, eager to add to the colonel's
body the trophy of our standard. As for me, I was still handing out powder and balls, the supply growing dangerously
low. I used the intervals to load and fire the harquebus
Rivas had left behind. I loaded it clumsily, for the weapon
was enormous in my hands, and it kicked like a mule, almost dislocating my shoulder. Even so, I got off at least five
or six shots. I would ram an ounce of lead into the muzzle,
carefully fill the pan with powder and place the cord in the
serpentine, concentrating on keeping the pan closed as I
blew on the cord, exactly as I had seen the captain and others do so many times. I had eyes only for the combat and
ears only for the thunder of the powder whose acrid black
smoke was burning my eyes, nostrils, and mouth. Angélica
de Alquézar's letter lay forgotten inside my doublet, next
to my heart.

"If I get out of this," Garrote growled as he hurried to
reload his harquebus, "I will never come back to Flanders,
not even for gold."

In the meantime, the battle continued at the walls of
the fort and on the dike below it. When he saw the men de-
serting Captain Fenice, who had died at the gate doing his
duty with great honor and integrity, Sergeant-Major don
Carlos Roma armed himself with a sword and buckler and
jumped into the path of the fleeing soldiers, attempting to

turn them back to the battle. He knew that the dike they had come along was narrow and that if he could slow the attackers, it would be possible to push them back. As they ran into each other, they would clog the road, and only those already there could fight. Thus, little by little, he was evening the battle on that front, and the Italians, now regrouped and with their courage renewed by their sergeant-major, were fighting with good heart, for men of that nation, when they have the will and good reason, know how to fight. They were driving the English away from the wall, halting the main attack.

Things were not going as well for us. A hundred English, in tight formation, were almost within reach of the terreplein, the fallen standard, and the gabions of the redoubt, hindered only by the significant damage our harquebusiers, spitting balls at them from less than twenty paces, continued to inflict.

"We're running out of powder!" I warned.

It was true. We had enough for only two or three more charges for each man. Curro Garote, cursing like a galley slave, slid down behind the parapet, his arm disabled by a musket ball. Pablo Olivares took over the Malagueño's two remaining shots, and continued to fire until he had exhausted those two and his own. Of the others, Juan Cuesta, from Gijón, had been dead for some time, sprawled between some gabions, and Antonio Sánchez, a veteran soldier from Tordesillas, was soon to join him. Fulgencio Puche, from Murcia, dropped with his hands to his face, bleeding through his fingers like a stuck pig. The remaining men fired their last shots.

"This is the end," said Pablo Olivares.

We looked at one another, undecided, hearing the cries of the English drawing closer up the slope. Their clamor was making me quake with terror, a bottomless despair. We had less time left than it takes to recite the Credo, and no options but the enemy or the swamp. Some men started drawing their swords.

"The standard," said Alatriste.

Several looked at him as if they did not understand his words. Others, Copons first among them, went and stood by the captain.

"He's right," said Mendieta. "Better with the standard."

I knew what he meant. Better out there with the standard, fighting around it, than here behind the gabions, cornered like rabbits. I no longer felt any fear, only a deep and ancient weariness, and a wish to finish this thing. I wanted to close my eyes and sleep for eternity. I noticed that the hair on my arms was standing on end as I reached back to unsheathe my dagger. Both hand and dagger were trembling, so I gripped it tightly. Alatriste saw me ready myself, and for a fraction of a second his gray-green eyes flashed with something that was both an apology and a smile. Then he bared his Toledo blade, threw off his hat and the belt with the twelve apostles, and without a word jumped up on the parapet.

"Spain! . . . Close in for Spain!" some yelled, following close behind.

"Not for Spain, no!" Garrote muttered, limping with his sword in his good hand. "My bollocks! Close in for my bollocks!"

I do not know how, but we survived. My recollections of the slope of the Terheyden redoubt are confused, just as they are for that hopeless assault. I know that we jumped to the top of the parapet, some quickly crossed themselves, and then, just as the nearest English were about to pick up our standard, we ran downhill like a pack of savage dogs, howling and brandishing our daggers and swords. They stopped short, terrorized by this unexpected aggression when they thought our resistance had been broken. They were still paralyzed, hands reaching out toward the staff of the flag, when we threw ourselves on them, killing at will. I fell upon the standard, clutching it in my arms, determined that no one would take it from me without first taking my life, and I rolled with it down the terreplein, over the bodies of a dead officer, Lieutenant Chacón, good old Rivas, and over the English that Alatriste and the others were slicing up as they descended the slope. We came with such momentum and ferocity—the strength of desperate men is that they do not expect salvation—that the English, demoralized by our assault and seeing the punishment they were taking, began to lose heart and fell back, tripping over one another. Then one turned his back, and others quickly followed suit. Captain Alatriste, Copons, the Olivares brothers, Garrote, and the others were red with enemy blood and blind from killing. Then, unexpectedly—exactly as I am telling you—the English began to run by the dozen, retreating, and our men were after them, wounding them from behind as they went on this way. They fought forward as far as the corpse of don Pedro de la Daga, then farther, leaving the ground behind them a slaughterhouse. I slipped and rolled down that bloody trail of butchered English with the standard held tightly in my arms, then followed, howling with all my might, hollering my despair, my rage, and the courage of the race of men and women who made me. As God is my witness, I was to know many more battles and combats, some as closely fought as this, but it is when I remember that day that I still burst out weeping like the boy I was, when I see myself barely fifteen years old, clutching that absurd piece of blue and white-checked linen, yelling and racing across the blood-soaked slope of the Terheyden redoubt. The day that Captain

Alatriste looked for a good place to die, and I, along with his comrades, followed him through the midst of the English troops because we were all going to die one way or other and because we would have been ashamed to let him go alone.

EPILOGUE

The rest is a painting, and it is history. It was already nine years later, when I crossed the street one morning to visit the studio of Diego Velázquez, who was Keeper of the Wardrobe to our lord and king in Madrid. It was a winter day, and an even more disagreeable gray than those days in Flanders. My spurred boots crunched through icy puddles, and despite the protective collar of my cape and the hat set firmly on my head, the cold wind was cutting into my face. I was grateful for the warmth of the dark corridor and, once in the large studio, for the fire happily blazing in the hearth. Large windows lit paintings hanging on the wall, displayed on easels, and stacked back to back on the parquet wood floor. The room smelled of paint, linseed oil, varnishes, and oil of turpentine, and also, deliciously, of chicken broth seasoned with spices and wine, which was simmering in a large kettle beside the hearth.

"Please serve yourself, señor Balboa," said Velázquez.

Since the day some eleven or twelve years ago that I first saw Velázquez on the steps of San Felipe, the most popular *mentidero,* or gossip spot, in Madrid, he had lost a good part of his Seville accent, owing, no doubt, to a trip to Italy, life at court, and the patronage of our king, Philip IV. At that moment he was engaged in meticulously cleaning his brushes with a cloth before lining them up on a table. He was dressed in a black jacket spattered with paint, his hair was unruly, and his mustache and goatee were uncombed. Our monarch's favorite painter never did his toilette until midmorning, when he interrupted his work to rest and fill his stomach after taking advantage of the early-morning light. None of those close to him dared bother him before that midmorning pause. Afterward, he would work a while longer, till the afternoon, when he enjoyed a light meal. Later, if pressing appointments or responsibilities at the palace did not require his presence, he would walk to San Felipe, the Plaza Mayor, or the Prado meadows, often in the company of don Francisco de Quevedo, Alonso Cano, and other friends, disciples, and acquaintances.

I deposited my cape, gloves, and hat on a footstool and went to the kettle, where I poured a dipperful into a glazed clay jug, warming my hands as I sipped it.

"How goes life at the palace?" I asked.

"Slowly."

We both laughed a little at the old joke. At the time, Velázquez was faced with the daunting task of furnishing paintings for the Hall of Realms in the new Buen Retiro palace. That and other graces had been granted directly by the king, and Velázquez was pleased to have them. It did, however, he sometimes lamented, rob him of the space and peace to work at his own pace. Which was why he had just passed on the duties of usher of the chamber to Juan Bautista del Mazo, as Velázquez was content to accept the honored but less demanding role of keeper of the wardrobe.

"And how is Captain Alatriste?" the painter inquired.

"Well. He sends you his greetings. He has gone to Calle de Francos with don Francisco de Quevedo and Captain Contreras to visit Lope at home."

"And how is our phoenix?"

"Poorly. The flight of his daughter Antoñita with Cristóbal Tenorio was a harsh blow. He has not yet recovered."

"I must find a free moment to visit him. Is he much worse then?"

"Everyone fears that he will not make it through this winter."

"A pity."

I drank a couple of sips more. The broth was scalding hot, but it was also reviving me.

"It seems there will be a war with Richelieu," Velázquez commented.

"That is what I have heard on the steps of San Felipe."

I went to set the jug on a table, and on the way I paused before a painting on an easel, which was finished, lacking only a coat of varnish. Angélica de Alquézar was breathlessly beautiful in Velázquez's portrait, dressed in white satin trimmed with gold frogs and tiny pearls, with a mantilla of Brussels lace around her shoulders. I knew it was from Brussels because I had given it to her. Her blue eyes stared out of the portrait with a sardonic gaze, and they seemed to follow my movements around the room, as in fact they had done through so many years of my life. Finding her here made me smile inside; it had been only hours since I left her, gaining the street just before dawn, muffled in my cape and with my hand on the hilt of my sword should her uncle's hired assassins be waiting for me. I still had her delicious fragrance on my fingertips, on my mouth and skin. I also had on my body the now-healed remembrance of her dagger, and in my thoughts her words of love and loathing, one as sincere as the other was deadly.

"I have brought you," I said to Velázquez, "a sketch of the Marqués de los Balbases' sword. An old comrade who saw it many times remembers it well."

I turned my back to Angélica's portrait. Then I took

out the paper I had folded inside my doublet and handed it to the painter.

"The grip was of bronze and hammered gold. Here, Your Mercy, you will see how the guards were fashioned."

Velázquez, who had put down his cloth and brushes, contemplated the sketch with a satisfied air.

"As for the plumes on his hat," I added, "they were undoubtedly white."

"Excellent," he said.

He put the paper on the table and looked at the painting, an expansive depiction of the surrender at Breda. It was destined to decorate the Hall of Realms and was enormous; here in the studio it hung on a special frame attached to the wall, with a ladder set before it so that Veláquez could work on the upper portion.

"I finally listened to you," he added, pensively. "Lances instead of standards."

It was I who had provided him with these details during long conversations we'd had in recent months, after don Francisco de Quevedo had suggested that my cooperation would be helpful in documenting the particulars of the scene. To accomplish his painting Diego Velázquez decided to dispense with the fury of combatants, the clash of steel—all the obligatory subject matter of traditional battle scenes—and instead sought serenity and grandeur. He wanted, as he told me more than once, to achieve a tone that was at once magnanimous and arrogant and also interpreted in the manner he painted: reality not like it was but as he depicted it, expressing things that conformed with truth but were not explicit, so that all the rest, the context and the spirit suggested by the scene, would be the work of the person who viewed it.

"What do you think of it?" he asked softly.

I knew perfectly well that he did not give a fig about my artistic judgment, especially coming, as it did, from a twenty-four-year-old soldier. He was asking for something different; I knew that from the way he was looking at me, not quite trusting and slightly calculating, as my eyes ran over the painting.

"It was like this and not like this," I said.

I regretted my words the minute they left my lips, for I was afraid I had offended him. But he limited himself to a faint smile.

"Good," he said. "I am aware that there is no hill of this height near Breda and that the perspective of the background is a little forced." He took a few steps and stood looking at the painting with his fists on his hips. "But the scene works, and that is what matters."

"I was not referring to those things."

"I know what you were referring to."

He went to the hand with which the Dutch Justin of Nassau was offering the key to our General Spínola—as yet

the key was no more than a sketch and a blob of color—
and rubbed it a little with his thumb. Then he stepped
back, never taking his eyes from the painting; he was focused on the space between their two heads, the area beneath the horizontal butt of the harquebus the soldier who
had neither beard nor mustache was carrying over his
shoulder, there where the aquiline profile of Captain Alatriste was hinted at, half hidden behind the officers.

"In the end," he said finally, "it will always be remembered as it is here. When you and I and all the rest of
them are dead."

I was studying the faces of the colonels and captains in
the foreground, some still lacking the artist's finishing
touches. Of least importance to me was that, except for
Justin of Nassau, the prince of Newburg, don Carlos
Coloma, the Marqués de Espinar, the Marqués de Leganés,
and Spínola himself, none of the other heads in the main
scene corresponded to those of royal personages. I was
equally indifferent to the fact that Velázquez had given the
features of his fellow artist and friend, Alonso Cano, to the
Dutch harquebusier on the left and that on the right he had
utilized features very close to his own for the officer in
high boots who was looking out toward the viewer. Nor
did I care that the chivalrous gesture of poor don Ambrosio Spínola—who had died in physical pain and shame
four years earlier, in Italy—was exactly the same as it had

been that morning, while the artist's rendering of the Dutch general attributed to him more humility and submission than Nassau had shown when he surrendered the city at Balanzón.

What I *had* been referring to was that in that serene composition—in that 'Please do not bow, Don Justin, no,' and in the restrained attitude of various officers—something was hidden that I, farther back among the lances but close enough to see clearly, had observed that day: the insolent pride of the conquerors and the ill will and hatred in the eyes of the conquered. The brutality with which we had killed one another and would still do so in the future assured that the graves that filled the landscape of the background amid the misty smoke from burning fires would never be enough to hold the dead.

As for who was in the foreground of the painting and who was not, one thing was certain: We, the loyal and long-suffering infantry were *not*. We, the old *tercios* that had done the dirty work in the mines and caponnieres, carried out *encamisada* raids in the night, breached the Sevenberge dike with fire and axes, fought at the Ruyter mill and the Terheyden fort; we foot soldiers with our rags and our worn-out weapons, our pustules, our illnesses, and our misery; we were nothing but cannon fodder. Yes, we were the eternal background against which the other Spain, the official Spain of laces and sweeping bows, took possession of the key to the city of Breda—which, as we had feared, we were not allowed to sack—and posed for posterity, indulging themselves in the sham, the luxury of showing a magnanimous spirit. We are among caballeros, and in Flanders the sun has not yet set.

"It will be a great painting," I said.

I was sincere. It would be a great painting, and the world would perhaps remember our unfortunate Spain, made resplendent in that canvas on which it was not difficult to sense the breath of immortality issuing from the palette of the greatest painter of the times we had known. The reality, however, my true memories, were to be found in the middle distance of the scene. Inadvertently, my glance kept straying there, beyond the central composition, which did not matter a nun's fart to me, to the old blue and white-checked standard on the shoulder of a bearer with thick hair and mustache, who well could be Lieutenant Chacón, whom I had watched die as he tried to save that same piece of cloth on the slope of the Terheyden redoubt. My eyes went to the harquebusiers—Rivas, Llop, and others who did not return to Spain or anywhere else for that matter—backs turned to the principal scene, lost in the forest of disciplined lances; the lancers themselves, all anonymous in the painting, were men to whom I could, one by one, give the names of the living and dead comrades who had carried those lances across Europe, holding them high with their sweat and their blood, to demonstrate the truth of what had been written.

Always on the brink of war
they fought, forever grand,
in Germany and Flanders, too,
in France and upon English land.
The very earth bowed down to them
trembling as they passed,
and ordinary soldiers, massed
in unparalleled campaign,
across the world, from East to West,
carried the sun of Spain.

It was they, Spaniards with several tongues and lands between them but all united in ambition, pride, and suffering, and not the pretentious figures portrayed in the foreground of the canvas, who were the ones to whom the Dutchman was delivering his precious key. To those nameless, faceless troops barely visible on the slope of a hill that never existed, where, at ten o'clock on the morning of 5 June in the twenty-fifth year of the century, regnant in Spain our king don Philip IV, I, along with Captain Alatriste, Sebastian Copons, Curro Garrote, and the remaining survivors of their decimated squad, witnessed the surrender of Breda. And nine years later, in Madrid, standing before Diego Velázquez's panorama, it seemed that I could again hear the drum and that I was watching, amid the forts and smoking trenches in the distance, near Breda, the slow advance of the old, implacable squads, the pikes and standards of what was the last and best infantry in the world: despised, cruel, arrogant Spaniards disciplined only when under fire, who suffered everything in any assault but would allow no man to raise his voice to them.

EDITOR'S NOTE CONCERNING THE PRESENCE OF CAPTAIN ALATRISTE IN DIEGO VELÁZQUEZ'S PAINTING OF *SURRENDER OF BREDA*

The alleged presence of Captain Diego Alatriste y Tenorio in the painting *Surrender of Breda* has been debated for many years. On the one hand we have the testimony of Íñigo Balboa, who was witness to the composition of the painting and who has unhesitatingly stated on two occasions (see p. 4 of *Captain Alatriste* and page 187 ms. in *Sun Over Breda)* that the captain is represented in Velázquez's canvas. On the other hand, studies of the heads on the right side have resulted in the positive identification of Spínola and established as probable those of Carlos Coloma, the Marqués de Leganés, the Marqués de Espinar, and the prince of Newburg, these according to analyses by professors Justi, Allende Salazar, Sánchez Cantón, and Temboury Álverez, but they reject the idea that any of the anonymous heads corresponds to the physical features Íñigo Balboa attributes to the captain.

The bearer holding the standard on his shoulder cannot be Diego Alatriste nor can the musketeer in the rear who has no beard or mustache. Similarly eliminated are the pale, bare-headed caballero standing beneath the standard and beside the horse, and the corpulent, dark-skinned, hatless officer standing beneath the horizontal butt of the harquebus, whom professor Sergio Zamorano from the University of Seville believes to be Captain Carmelo Bragado. Some scholars have argued the possibility that Alatriste was portrayed in the officer on the extreme right, behind the horse, looking toward the viewer, a person other experts, such as Temboury, judge to be Velázquez himself, who thus balanced the supposed inclusion of his friend Alonso Cano at the extreme left as the Dutch harquebusier.

Professor Zamorano similarly points out in his study of the painting, *Breda: realidad y leyenda*, that Diego Alatriste's physical attributes might correspond to those of the officer situated at the right of the canvas, although that man's features, he suggests, are softer than those described by Íñigo Balboa when he speaks of Captain Alatriste. In any case, as the translator and scholar Miguel Antón of Barcelona writes in his essay *"El Capitán Alatriste y la rendición de Bredá,"* the age of that caballero, no more than thirty or so, does not coincide with the age of Alatriste in 1625, much less with his fifty-one or fifty-two years in 1634–1635, the date the painting was completed. Neither does the clothing of the officer correspond with what Alatriste, then a simple soldier with the nominal rank of squad corporal, would be wearing in Flanders. There is still the possibility that Alatriste was not represented in the group on the right but among the Spaniards down the slope, in the center of the painting, behind the extended arm of General Spínola. However, a very careful examination of their features and clothing published in *Figaro* magazine by the specialist Etienne de Montety seems to negate that theory.

And yet, Íñigo Balboa's affirmation on page four of the first volume in this series sounds unequivocal: ". . . because later, on the bulwarks of Julich, my father was killed by a ball from a harquebus, which is why Diego Velázquez did not include him in his painting of the *Surrender of Breda* as he did his friend and fellow Diego Alatriste, who is indeed there, behind the horse." These disconcerting words were for a long time considered by most experts to be less factual than a gratuitous affirmation—Balboa's exaggerated homage to his beloved Captain Alatriste—with no basis in truth. Balboa was a soldier in Flanders and Italy, a standard bearer and lieutenant in Roicroi, lieutenant of the royal mails and captain of the Guardia Española of King Philip IV before retiring for personal reasons around 1660 at the age of fifty. That was following his marriage to doña Inés Álvarez of Toledo, the widowed Marquesa de Alguazas, and his later disappearance from public life. His memoirs came to light only in 1951, in an auction of books and manuscripts in the Claymore house in London. Arturo Pérez-Reverte used the memoirs as his documented source for *The Adventures of Captain Alatriste,* and he confesses that for a long time he believed that Íñigo's assertion that Diego Alatriste did in fact appear in Velázquez's painting was false.

But chance has finally resolved the mystery, disclosing data that had been overlooked by scholars and by the author of this series of novels based almost entirely on Balboa's original manuscript.[1] In August 1998, when I visited Pérez-Reverte in his home near El Escorial to clear up some editorial matters, he confided to me a discovery he had made accidentally as he was documenting the epilogue of the third volume of the series. Only the day before, while consulting José Camón Aznar's *Velázquez*—one of the more definitive works on the author of *Surrender of Breda*—Pérez-Reverte had come upon something that had left him stupefied. On pages 508 and 509 of the first volume (Madrid: Espasa Calpe, 1964), professor Camón Aznar confirmed that an X-radiographic study of the canvas had validated some of Íñigo Balboa's affirmations concerning the Velázquez painting that had at first seemed to be contradictory, such as the fact, proved on the X-ray plate, that the artist had originally painted standards instead of

[1]I*Papeles del alférez Balboa* (Lieutenant Balboa's Papers). Manuscript of 478 pages, Madrid, undated. Sold by the Claymore auction house in London, 25 November, 1952. Presently located in the Biblioteca Nacional. (Editor's note)

lances, not unusual in a painter famous for his pentimentos (modifications made along the way that led him to change outlines, alter compositions, and eliminate objects and persons already painted). In addition to the standards being replaced by lances, the horse on the Spaniards' side was suggested in three different attitudes; in the background, in the correct geographical orientation, toward the Sevenberge dike and the sea, there appears to be an expanse of water and a ship; Spínola was sketched in a more erect position; and, on the Spanish side, it is possible to make out the heads and embroidered collars of additional personages. For reasons we cannot divine, in the definitive version Velázquez overpainted the head of a man who appears to be a noble and also possibly another. And there is something more: In regard to Diego Alatriste's presence, which Íñigo Balboa describes as he views the canvas and specifies his exact location—*the area beneath the horizontal butt of the harquebus that the soldier without a beard or mustache was carrying over his shoulder*—the viewer sees only empty space above the blue doublet of a pike man whose back is turned.

The true surprise, however—proof that painting, like literature, is but a succession of enigmas and closed envelopes that enclose other closed envelopes—is buried in half a line on page 509 of Camón Aznar's book and refers to that same, very suspicious and empty space where the

X-ray revealed that "Behind that head one can make out another with an aquiline profile . . ."

Reality often amuses itself by confirming on its own what seems to us to be fiction. We do not know why Velázquez later decided to eliminate from his masterpiece a head he had already painted. Perhaps later books in this series will clarify that mystery.[2] But now, almost four cen-

---

[2]The disappearance *a posteriori* of the two most documented references to Captain Diego Alatriste y Tenorio known to this time is extraordinary. While the testament of Íñigo Balboa and the study of the painting *Surrender of Breda* by Velázquez prove that the captain's image was, for unknown reasons, erased from the canvas on a date later than winter of 1634, we have a first version of a play by Pedro Calderón de la Barca entitled *The Siege of Bredá*, and in it, too, there are signs of later manipulation. This first complete version, contemporaneous to the date of the first performance of the play in Madrid—which was written around 1626—and coinciding along general lines with the manuscript copy of the original made by Diego López de Mora in 1632, contains some forty lines that were suppressed in the definitive version. In them explicit reference is made to the death of Colonel don Pedro de la Daga and to the defense of the Terheyden redoubt carried out by Diego Alatriste, whose name is quoted two times in the text. The original fragment, discovered by Professor Klaus Oldenbarnevelt of the Instituto de Estudios Hispánicos in the University of Utrecht, is housed in the archive and library of the Duques del Nuevo Extremo in Seville, and we reproduce it in the appendix at the end of this volume with the kind permission of doña Macarena Bruner de Lebrija, Duquesa del Nuevo Extremo. What is odd is that those forty lines disappear in the canonical version of the work published in 1636 in Madrid by José Calderón, brother of the author, in *Primera parte de Comedias de don Pedro Calderón de la Barca*. The reason for Alatriste's disappearance in the play about the siege of Breda, as well as in the Velázquez painting, has not to this date been explained. Unless it was in response to

turies after all that happened, we know that Íñigo Balboa did not lie and that Captain Alatriste was—and still is— on the canvas of *Surrender of Breda*.

—The Editor

an express order attributable perhaps to King Philip IV or, more likely, the Conde Duque de Olivares, whose disfavor Diego Alatriste may have incurred, again for reasons unknown to us, between 1634 and 1636.

A SELECTION FROM

A POETRY BOUQUET

BY VARIOUS LIVELY MINDS

OF THIS CITY

🌸

Printed in the XVII century, lacking the printer's mark, and
conserved in the "Condado de Guadalmedina" Section of the
Nuevo Extremo Ducal Archive and Library, Seville

DON FRANCISCO DE QUEVEDO

Inscription to the Marqués Ambrosio Spínola
Commander of Catholic Forces in Flanders

Sinon, Ulysses, and the Trojan Horse
Won the day in Troy with treachery,
Whereas in Ostende, leading your troops,
It was your sword that crushed the enemy.

As your squads approached their walls
Frisia and Breda foresaw their destiny;
Facing your might, the heretic gave way
His banners struck, his pennon a mockery.

You subjected the Palatinate,
To benefit the Spanish monarchy,
Your ideals countering their heresy.

In Flanders, we badly missed your gallantry,
E'en more in Italy . . . and now this eulogy
Amid sorrow we dare not contemplate.

THE CABALLERO OF THE YELLOW DOUBLET

TO IÑIGO BALBOA, IN HIS LATER YEARS

'Pon my oath, no difference can I find
'Twixt the young Basque known for his diligence
And the hidalgo once a Flanders soldier:
That lad gave good account of his existence.

Hearing tales about your dashing swordsman,
The orb, envisioning that experience,
The flashing blade, the valiant adventure,
With military tears bemoans his absence.

His valor was your fortune and your glory,
And wonder at the days you lived with him
Will be the one reaction to your story.

Because of you, thwarting oblivion,
His memory will not be lost through time:
Diego de Alatriste, Capitán!

DEFENSE OF THE GARRISON AT TERHEYDEN:
AN EXCERPT FROM ACT III OF THE FAMOUS PLAY
THE DEFENSE OF BREDA

Don Pedro Calderón de la Barca

D. FADRIQUE BAZÁN:

Oh, if only Henry would march
This way, engage the Spanish
In this place, a happy day
It would be for our intentions!

D. VINCENTE PIMENTEL:

We are not so fortunate, señor,
As to be granted such a blessing.

ALONSO LADRÓN, CAPTAIN:

I would venture that he will join
With those fat *flinflones*, the German guard,
With whom he is comfortably allied.
We are told that when they hear our
"Santiago! Close in for Spain!"
Even though they know the name
And know he is our patron saint
And one apostle of the twelve,
They believe we call the devil,
And that without discrimination
We summon devils as well as saints,
And that all come to our aid.

D. FRANCISCO DE MEDINA:

> If Henry leads his troops along
> The Antwerp road, the Italians
> Will be waiting to engage him.

The bugle sounds "To Arms"

D. FADRIQUE:

> It seems that they are readying
> For battle.

ALONSO:

> > > God's bones!
>
> It will be these same Italians
> Who glory in the occasion
> While we Spanish will be watching
> Without a fight!

D. FADRIQUE:

> > > *Say not so!*
>
> *Allow Colonel de la Daga*
> *To choose for you a number*
> *Of the loyal men of Spain*
> *That in the furor of the battle*
> *They may show what swordplay is!*

DON GONZALO FDZ. DE CÓRDOBA:

> *They would disobey?*

DON FADRIQUE:

> > > *Not at all!*
>
> *This is a place and time in which*

The man who does not draw his blade
Will cease to call himself a man,
And less, a Spaniard.

D. GONZALO:

          Obedience

Is in war what most confines
And makes a prison for a soldier:
More praise and more renown are won
By one who docilely endures
Than by fervor in the fray.

D. FADRIQUE:

But were the greater glory not
Obedience, what prisons would
There be that could contain us?

ALONSO:

Withal, these Flemish caballeros
Should not draw my ire, for
If the tercios be broken,
I shall have to fight today.
Though I be hanged tomorrow.

Drum rolls

D. VICENTE:

Either way is an offense!

Drum rolls

D. FADRIQUE:

How fine the voices of the drums
And trumpets sound accompanying
The stirring cadence of the cannon!

D.F. DE MEDINA:

By heaven, the enemy has fought through
The Walloons' last defense!

Drum rolls

D. FADRIQUE:

And now draw nigh the Italian lines!

ALONSO:

Oh, those accursed flinflones.
*When our friends combat that foe
Their squads will not prevail.*

D. GONZALO:

Look, there, see de la Daga . . .

Aside

ALONSO:

(Slanderously, Jiñalasoga)

D. GONZALO:

See how proudly he succumbs
Along with his brave Spaniards,
Resisting to the very end.

Drum rolls

DON FADRIQUE:

I am so schooled and practiced in
The matter of obedience
That when I hear that first command,
My blade lies quiet in its sheath!
They say the man who stands in place
Rather than fight, is the one who
Better fulfills his obligations!

D. VICENTE:

The garrison now lies in ruins.
Do you not hear the voices?
By God, I now believe that
He will enter the town tonight!

ALONSO:

How mean you?

D. FADRIQUE:

The town?
Obedience will forgive me,
He must not enter.

D. VICENTE:

Let us attack,
Whether the general be discontented
Or resigned.

D. GONZALO:

Oh, caballeros,

Lose everything, but do not counter
Your instructions.

D. FADRIQUE:

We do not fail
Our obligations, but there are times
That force a different effort, when
An order broken is not broken.

D. VICENTE:

But, look, there, attend the action,
What one man daringly attempts.
Muted, the wind stops blowing,
The sun is halted in its path.
Do you not see the Italian
Sergeant-Major, standing against
Henry's boldly advancing army?
With his cries he animates
His gallant men, and together
They forestall the squads
Of the enemy. We must give
This triumph an eternal name:
Carlos Roma, you are most worthy,
Deserving that your king should
Honor you with New World lands,
With appointments, and with glory.
And now with sword and buckler, soldiers
Are erupting onto the field.
And following their example, the Italians

Spring into action. Let them
Enjoy the glory and it be we
Who witness. For here our envy may be
Seen as noble, as too our praise.
Spain, which in far greater number
Has been victorious in her battles,
Has no reason to omit
The name of Italy from this triumph,
For it is they who are the victors.

D. FCO DE MEDINA

There is another victory
Before us, another triumph,
Which is the rescue of our banner
From capture and from offense.
This has been done by those few
Brave and valiant Spaniards, they
Who here escorted Colonel
De la Daga, and who restrained
So fiercely the English troops with their
Amazing, brash, and bold assault.

D. GONZALO:

Who was he, then, who led them,
Fierce Mars and noble Hector?

ALONSO:

Diego Alatriste y Tenorio,
The "Captain" is an honorary

Title, fittingly won amid
The clamor and the roar of cannon.

D. GONZALO:

On such an august day as this
May Alatriste in renown
Yield only to brave Carlos Roma.
Who, along with his men,
The king will generously reward
For being victors in Terheyden.

D. FADRIQUE:

In defeat and disarray.
The Flemish are retreating, fleet
As the wind; and now all honor
Falls to the victors, may their
Noble brows be crowned with laurel,
And on a thousand plaques of bronze
Eternally their feat shall live,
Reaching the limits of the orb.

It must be noted that the verses in italics have been taken from the original manuscript, as they were not included in *Primera parte de comedias de don Pedro Calderón de la Barca*, collected by don Joseph, Calderón's brother, and printed in Madrid in the year 1636. Why the poet later chose to delete those lines has not been determined.